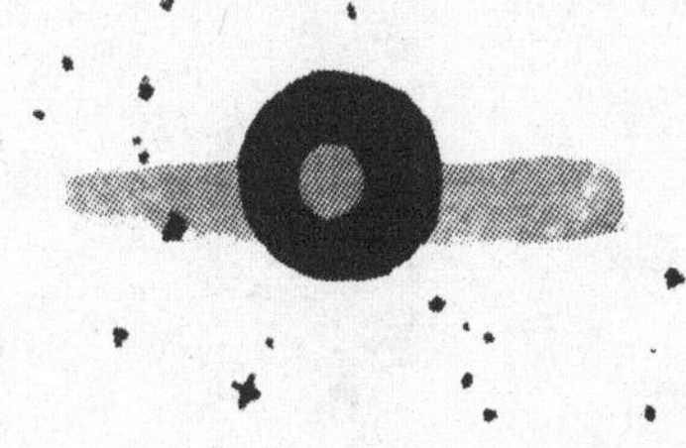

ALEXEI TOLSTOI

AELITA

Fredonia Books
Amsterdam, The Netherlands

Aelita

by
Alexei Tolstoy

ISBN: 1-58963-374-1

Reprinted from the original edition

Fredonia Books
Amsterdam, The Netherlands
http://www.fredoniabooks.com

In order to make original editions of historical works available to scholars at an economical price, this facsimile of the original edition is reproduced from the best available copy and has been digitally enhanced to improve legibility, but the text remains unaltered to retain historical authenticity.

CONTENTS

A STRANGE NOTICE

A strange notice appeared in Krasniye Zori Street. It was written on a small sheet of grey paper, and nailed to the peeling wall of a deserted building. Walking past the house, Archibald Skiles, the American newspaper correspondent, saw a barefoot young woman in a neat cotton-print frock standing before the notice and reading it with her lips. Her tired, sweet face showed no surprise; her blue eyes, with a little fleck of madness in them, were unmoved. She tucked a lock of wavy hair behind her ear, lifted her basket of vegetables and crossed the street.

As it happened, the notice merited greater attention. His curiosity aroused, Skiles read it, moved closer, rubbed his eyes, and read it again.

"Twenty-three," he muttered at last, which was his way of saying, "I'll be damned!"

The notice read as follows:

"Engineer M. S. Los invites all who wish to fly with him to the planet of Mars on August 18, to call on him between 6 and 8 p.m. at 11, Zhdanovskaya Embankment."

It was written as simply as that, in indelible pencil.

Skiles felt his pulse. It was normal. He glanced at his watch. The time was ten past four of August 17, 192. . . .

Skiles had been prepared for anything in that crazy city, but not for this, not the notice on the peeling wall. It unnerved him.

The wind swept down the empty street. The big houses with their broken and boarded windows, seemed untenanted. Not a single head showed in them. The young woman across the street put down her basket and stared at Skiles. Her sweet face was calm but weary.

Skiles bit his lip. He pulled out an old envelope and jotted down Los's address. While he was thus engaged, a tall, broad-shouldered man, a soldier, to judge by his clothes—a beltless tunic and puttees—stopped by the notice. He had no cap on, and his hands were thrust idly into his pockets. The back of his strong neck tensed as he read.

"Here's a man—taking a swing at Mars!" he muttered with unconcealed admiration, turning his tanned, cheerful face to Skiles. There was a scar across his temple. His eyes were a grey-brown, with little flecks in them, like those of the barefoot woman. (Skiles had long since noted these curious flecks in Russian eyes, had even mentioned the fact in one of his articles, to wit: "... the absence of stability in their eyes, now mocking, now fanatically resolute, and lastly, that baffling expression of superiority—is highly painful to the European.")

"I've a good mind to fly with him—as simple as that," he said, looking Skiles up and down with a good-natured smile.

Then he narrowed his eyes. His smile vanished. He had noticed the woman standing across the street beside her basket. Jerking up his chin, he called to her:

"What are you doing there, Masha?" (She blinked her eyes rapidly.) "Get along home." (She shifted her small dusty feet, sighed, hung her head.) "Get along, I say, I'll be home soon."

The woman picked up her basket and walked away.

"I've been demobbed, you know—shell-shocked and wounded. Spend my time reading notices—bored stiff," the soldier said.

"Are you going to see this man?" Skiles inquired.

"Certainly."

"But it's preposterous—flying fifty million kilometres through space....

"Yes. It is pretty far."

"The man's a fraud—or a raving lunatic."

"You never can tell."

It was Skiles who narrowed his eyes now as he studied the soldier. There it was, that mocking expression, that baffling look of superiority. He flushed with anger and stalked off in the direction of the Neva River. He strode along confidently, with long swinging steps. In the park he sat on a bench, shoved his hand into his pocket where, like the inveterate smoker and man of business that he was, he kept his tobacco shreds, filled his pipe with a jab of his thumb, lit up, and stretched out his legs.

The full-grown lime-trees sighed overhead. The air was warm and damp. A little boy, naked except for a dirty polka-dot shirt, was sitting on a sand-pile. He looked as though he had been there for hours. The wind ruffled his soft flaxen hair. He was holding a string to which the leg of an ancient, draggle-tailed crow was tied. The crow looked sullen and cross, and, like the boy, glared at Skiles.

Suddenly—for the fraction of a second—he felt dizzy. His head whirled. Was he dreaming? Was all this—the boy, the crow, the empty houses, deserted streets, strange glances, and that little notice inviting him to Mars—was it all a dream?

Skiles took a long draw at his strong tobacco, unfolded his map of Petrograd and traced the way to Zhdanovskaya Embankment with the stem of his pipe.

THE WORKSHOP

Skiles walked into a yard littered with rusty iron scrap and empty cement barrels. Sickly blades of grass grew on the piles of rubbish, between tangled coils of wire and broken machine parts. The dusty windows of a tall shed at the far end of the yard reflected the setting sun. In its low doorway a worker sat mixing red lead in a bucket. Skiles asked for Engineer Los. The man jerked his head towards the shed. Skiles entered.

The shed was dimly lit. An electric bulb covered with a tin cone hung over a table piled with technical drawings and books. A tangle of scaffolding rose ceiling-high at the back of the shed. There was a blazing forge, fanned by another worker. Skiles saw the studded metal surface of a spheric body gleaming through the scaffolding. The crimson rays of the setting sun and the dark clouds rising from the sea were framed in the open gate outside.

"Someone here to see you," said the worker at the forge.

A broad-shouldered man of medium height emerged from behind the scaffolding. His thick crop of hair was white, his face young and clean-shaven, with a large handsome mouth and piercing, light-grey, unblinking eyes. He wore a soiled homespun shirt open at the throat, and patched trousers held up by a piece of twine. There was a stained drawing in his hand. As he approached Skiles he fumbled at his throat in a vain attempt to button his shirt.

"Is it about the notice? D'you want to fly?" he asked in a husky voice. He offered Skiles a chair under the electric bulb, sat down facing him, laid his drawing on the table, and filled his pipe. It was Engineer Mstislav Sergeyevich Los.

Lowering his eyes, he struck a match. Its flame illumined his keen face, the two bitter lines near his mouth, the broad sweep of his nostrils and his long dark eyelashes. Skiles liked that face. He said he had no intention of flying to Mars but that he had read the notice in Krasniye Zori Street, and deemed it his duty to inform his readers of so extraordinary and sensational a project as Los's interplanetary trip.

Los heard him out, his unblinking eyes fixed on his face.

"Pity you won't fly with me. A great pity!" He shook his head. "People shy away from me the moment I mention the subject. I expect to take off in four days and haven't found a companion yet." He struck another match, and blew out a cloud of smoke.

"What d'you want to know?"

"The story of your life."

"It can be of no interest to anybody," said Los. "There's nothing remarkable about it. I went to school on a pittance and shifted for myself since I was twelve. My youth, my studies, and my work—there's nothing in them to interest your readers, nothing—except ..." Los frowned and set his mouth, "this contraption." He jabbed his pipe at the scaffolding. "I've been working on it a long time. Started building two years ago. That's all."

"How many months d'you expect it to take you to reach Mars?" Skiles asked, studying the point of his pencil.

"Nine or ten hours, I think. Not more."

"Oh!" Skiles reddened. His mouth twitched.

"I would be very much obliged," he began with studied politeness, "if you were to trust me more, and treat our interview seriously."

Los put his elbows on the table and enveloped himself in a cloud of smoke. His eyes gleamed through the haze.

"On August 18, Mars will be forty million kilometres away from the Earth. This is the distance I shall have to fly. First, I shall have to get through the layer of the Earth's atmosphere, which is 75 kilometres. Second, the space between the planets, which is 40 million kilometres. Third, the layer of the Martian atmosphere—65 kilometres. It is only those 140 kilometres of atmosphere that matter."

He rose and dug his hands into his trouser pockets. His head was in the shadow. All Skiles saw was his exposed chest and hairy arms with the rolled up shirt-sleeves.

"Flight is usually associated with a bird, a falling leaf, or a plane. But these do not really fly. They float. In the strict sense of the word, flight is the drop of a body propelled by the force of gravity. Take a rocket. In space, where there is no resistance, where there is nothing to obstruct its flight, a rocket travels with increasing velocity. I am likely to approach the velocity of light if no magnetic influences interfere. My machine is built on the rocket principle. I shall have to pierce 140 kilometres of terrestrian and Martian atmosphere. This will take an hour and a half, including the take-off and landing. Add another hour for climbing out of the Earth's gravitational field. Once I am in space, I shall be able to fly at any speed I like. There are just two dangers. One is that my blood vessels might burst from excessive acceleration, and the other, that the machine might hit the Martian atmosphere at too great a speed. It would be like striking sand. The machine and everything in it would turn into gas. Particles of planets, of unborn or perished worlds, hurtle through interstellar space. Whenever they enter the atmosphere they burn up. Air is an almost impenetrable shield, although apparently it was pierced at one time on our planet."

Los pulled his hand out of his pocket, laid it on the table under the light and clenched his fist.

"In Siberia, amid the eternal ice, I dug up mammoths that had perished in the cracks of the earth. I found grass in their teeth—they had once grazed in regions now bound by ice. I ate their meat. They had not decomposed, frozen as they were and buried in snow. The Earth's axis had apparently deflected very abruptly. The Earth either collided with some celestial body, or we had a second satellite revolving round us, smaller than the moon. The Earth must have attracted it, and it collided with the Earth and shifted its axis. It could very well have been this impact that destroyed the continent in the Atlantic Ocean lying west of Africa. To avoid disintegrating when I rocket into the Martian atmosphere, I shall have to keep down my speed. This is why I allow six or seven hours for the flight in outer space. In a few years travelling to Mars will be as simple as flying, say, from Moscow to New York."

Los stepped away from the table and threw an electric switch. Arc lights went on, hissing overhead under the ceiling. Skiles saw drawings, diagrams and maps pinned on the board walls, shelves loaded with optical and measuring instruments, spacesuits, stacks of tinned food, fur clothes and a telescope on a dais in the corner.

Los and Skiles walked over to the scaffolding built round the metal egg. Skiles estimated that it was roughly 8 1/2 metres high and 6 metres in diameter. A flat steel belt ran round its middle, projecting over its lower part like an umbrella. This was the parachute brake to increase the machine's resistance during its drop through the atmosphere. There were three portholes under the parachute. The bottom of this egg-like machine terminated in a narrow neck girdled by a double spiral of massive steel—the buffer to absorb the shock during the landing.

Tapping his pencil on the riveted shell, Los embarked on a detailed description of his interplanetary ship. It was built of pliable refractory steel, fortified from within with ribs and lightweight framework. So much for the outer casing. Inside it was a second casing made of six layers of rubber, felt and leather, which contained observation instruments and various appliances, such as oxygen tanks, carbonic acid absorbers, and shock-absorbent containers for instruments and provisions. Special "peepholes" made of short metal tubes and prismatic glasses projected beyond the outer casing.

The propulsion mechanism was installed in the spiral-choked neck made of a steel harder than astronomical bronze. Vertical canals were drilled in it, each of which broadened at the top to issue into a detonation chamber. The chambers were equipped with spark plugs and feeders. Just as gasolene is fed to a motor, ultralyddite, a fine powder of unusual explosive force, was fed to the detonation chambers. Discovered by a Petrograd factory, ultralyddite was more powerful than any other known explosive. The jet produced by the explosive was cone-shaped and had an exceedingly narrow base. To ensure that the axis of the jet coincided with the axis of the vertical canals of the neck, the ultralyddite fed to the detonation chambers was first passed through a magnetic field.

This was the general principle of the propulsion mechanism. It was a rocket. Its supply of ultralyddite would last for 100 hours. The velocity of the machine was regulated by decreasing or increasing the number of detonations per second. Its lower part was much heavier than the upper, which would cause it to turn neck foremost towards the field of gravitation.

"Who financed your project?" asked Skiles.

Los looked surprised.

"Why, the Republic...."

The two went back to the table. After a moment's silence, Skiles asked somewhat uncertainly:

"D'you think you'll find any living beings on Mars?"

"I'll have an answer to that on Friday morning, August 19."

"I offer you ten dollars per line of your travel notes. You can have the money in advance for six articles of 200 lines each, the check to be cashed in Stockholm. How about it?"

Los laughed and nodded. Skiles perched on a corner of the table to write out the check.

"Pity you won't come with me. It's really a short trip. Shorter, in fact, than hiking from here to Stockholm," said Los, puffing on his pipe.

A FELLOW-TRAVELLER

Los stood leaning against the gatepost. His pipe was cold.

Beyond the gate, an empty lot stretched all the way to the bank of the Zhdanovka. On the other side of the river loomed the blurred outlines of trees on Petrovsky Island, tinged by the melancholy sunset. Wisps of clouds, touched by the sun's glow, were scattered like islands in the expanse of greenish sky, studded with a few twinkling stars. All was quiet on old Mother Earth.

Kuzmin, the worker who had been mixing red lead, strolled up to the gate. He flicked his burning cigarette into the darkness.

"It isn't easy, parting with the Earth," he said softly. "It's hard enough leaving home. You keep looking back as you pack off to the railway station. My house may have a thatch roof, but it's mine, and there's no place like home. As for leaving the Earth—"

"The kettle's boiling," said Khokhlov, the other worker. "Come, Kuzmin, and have your tea."

Kuzmin sighed. "Yes, that's that," he said, retracing his steps to the forge. Sullen Khokhlov and Kuzmin sat on a couple of crates. They carefully broke their bread, picked the bones out of the sun-cured fish and chewed it unhurriedly. Jerking his beard, Kuzmin said in an undertone:

"I'm sorry for the old man. There aren't many like him in the world."

"He isn't dead yet, is he?"

"A flyer told me he climbed close to eight versts—it was summer, mind you—and his oil froze. Can you imagine what it is like higher up? Must be ice-cold, and pitch dark."

"What I say is, he isn't dead yet," Khokhlov repeated sullenly.

"There isn't a soul who wants to fly with him. Nobody believes him. The notice has been up on the wall for over a week."

"I believe him."

"You think he'll get there?"

"He will. And they'll sit up and take notice in Europe then."

"Who'll sit up?"

"They'll sit up, I'm telling you. And they'll have to like it or lump it. Who'll Mars belong to, eh?—the Soviets."

"Why, that'd be great!"

Kuzmin made room on his crate for Los. The engineer sat down and took up a tin mug of steaming tea.

"Won't you fly with me, Khokhlov?"

"No," Khokhlov said. "I'm scared."

Los smiled, took a sip of his tea and turned to Kuzmin.

"What about you, my friend?"

"I'd be glad to, but my wife is a sick woman, and then there are the children. Can't very well leave them, can I?"

"Yes, it seems I'll have to fly alone," said Los, setting down the empty mug and wiping his lips with his hand. "Volunteers are scarce." He smiled again and shook his head. "A girl came to see me about it yesterday. 'I'll come with you,' she said. 'I'm nineteen; I can sing, dance and play the guitar, and I want to leave the Earth—I'm sick of all these revolutions. Will I need an exit visa?' After our little talk she sat down and cried. 'You cheated me,' she wailed, 'I thought it was much nearer.' Then there was a young man. He spoke in a deep bass voice and had moist hands. 'D'you take me for an idiot?' he boomed. 'You can't fly to Mars. How dare you hang up such notices?' It was all I could do to pacify him."

Los rested his elbows on his knees and gazed at the coals. His face looked tired and drawn. He seemed to be relaxing after a long strain. Kuzmin went to get some tobacco. Khokhlov coughed.

"Aren't you scared at all?"

Los turned on him his eyes warmed by the flaming coals.

"No, I'm not. I'm sure I'll make it. And if I don't, the end will be too swift to be painful. There's something else that worries me. Suppose I miscalculate and miss the Martian field of gravitation. My supplies of fuel, oxygen and food will last for a long time. And there I'll be flying in the dark, with a star shining somewhere ahead. A thousand years from now my frozen corpse will plunge into its fiery oceans. Just think of my corpse flying through obscurity for a thousand years! And the long days of anguish when I'll still breathe—I'll live for days and days in that box, all alone in the universe! It isn't dying that scares me, but the solitude, the hopeless solitude in eternal obscurity. That's the thing I'm afraid of. I'd hate to fly by myself."

Los stared at the coals with narrowed eyes, his mouth set obstinately.

Kuzmin appeared in the door and called softly:

"Someone to see you."

"Who is it?" Los rose to his feet.

"A Red Army man."

Kuzmin came in, followed by the man in the beltless tunic who had read the notice in Krasniye Zori Street. He nodded to Los, glanced at the scaffolding, and approached the table.

"Need a travelling companion?"

Los offered him a chair and sat down facing him.

"Yes, I'm looking for someone to come with me to Mars."

"I know—I read the notice. I had a man show me the star in the sky. It's a long way. What are the terms—the pay and keep?"

"Are you a family man?"

"I've got a wife, but no children."

He drummed on the table with his fingers and inspected the shed curiously. Los told him briefly about the flight, and warned him about the risk. He promised to provide for his wife, and said he would give him his wages in advance, in cash and provisions. The Red Army man nodded absently.

"Do you know what we'll find there? Men or monsters?"

Los scratched the back of his head and laughed.

"There ought to be people—something like us. We'll see when we get there. It's like this—for some years now, the big radio stations in Europe and America have been receiving strange undecipherable signals. They were first thought to be caused by magnetic storms. But they were too much like alphabetic signals. Someone is trying to contact us. Who can it be? As far as we know, there's no life on any of the planets, outside Mars. That's the only place the signals can come from. Look at its map—it's covered with a network of canals (he pointed to a drawing of Mars nailed to the wall). They seem to have a very powerful radio station. Mars is calling the Earth. So far, we have been unable to reply. But we can fly there. It is scarcely possible that the radio stations on Mars were built by monsters or creatures unlike us. Mars and the Earth are two tiny globes revolving in close proximity. The laws are the same for both of us. The dust of life flies about the universe. The same spores settle on Mars and the Earth, and all the myriad frozen stars. Life appears everywhere, and it is governed everywhere by man-like creatures. There is no animal more perfect than man."

"I'm coming with you," said the Red Army man resolutely. "When do I bring my things?"

"Tomorrow. I must show you round the ship. Your name?"

"Alexei Ivanovich Gusev."

"Occupation?"

Gusev glanced at Los absent-mindedly, then lowered his eyes to his fingers tapping the table.

"I've been to school," he said, "I know something about motor-cars, flew a plane as an observer, fought in the war since I was eighteen. That's my story in a nutshell. I was wounded several times, and am now in the reserve." Suddenly he rubbed the crown of his head savagely and laughed. "The things I've been through in the last seven years! To tell the truth, I ought to have had the command of a regiment by now—but I'm too hot-headed. As soon as the fighting died down I'd grow restless—couldn't wait till we were in the fray again. I'd go off my rocket—ask to be sent on an assignment, or simply run away." (He rubbed his head again and grinned.) "I founded four republics—can't recall the cities now, and one time I rallied something like three hundred chaps to go and liberate India. But we got lost in the hills on the way, were caught in a storm and a landslide. Our horses were all done for. Few of us got back. Then I spent two months with Makhno—felt like going on a spree. But the bandits were a bit too thick for me—I joined the Red Army. Chased the

Poles out of Kiev all the way to Warsaw with Budyonny's cavalry. Got wounded the last time, when we stormed Perekop, and was laid up for about a year. When I left hospital I didn't know what to do with myself. Then I met this girl of mine, and married her. She's a good soul. I've a soft spot for her, but I can't stay at home. And there's no point in going back to the village—my folks are all dead and the land's gone to seed. Nothing to do in town either. The war is over, and it's not likely we'll have another one soon. Take me on, Mstislav Sergeyevich. I might come in handy out there, on Mars."

"Good," said Los. He shook Gusev's hand. "See you tomorrow."

A SLEEPLESS NIGHT

Everything was ready for the take-off. But the two men scarcely slept the next two days, stowing away countless trifles in the spaceship's containers. They tested the instruments, tore down the scaffolding, and pulled part of the roof out in the shed.

Los introduced Gusev to the propulsion mechanism and the key instruments. His travelling companion, he saw, was both intelligent and shrewd.

They fixed the hour of their departure for 6 p.m. the following day.

Late at night, Los sent Gusev and the workers away. He put out all the lights but one and lay down fully dressed on the iron cot behind the telescope in the corner.

It was a quiet, starry night. Los did not sleep. He clasped his hands behind his head and stared into the dark. He had had no chance to relax for days and days. But this last night on Earth he'd let himself go: weep, man, weep and torment yourself.

Painful memories came flooding in, memories of a semi-dark room, a candle shaded by a book. The air heavy with the smell of medicine. A basin on the rug by the bed. Every time he got up and stepped past it, blurred shadows danced on the dreary wallpaper. His heart gave a twist. There, on the bed, lay Katya, the dearest thing in his life, his wife—her breath coming in quiet, short gasps. Her thick, tangled hair spread over the pillow, and her knees were raised under the quilt. Katya was leaving him. Her gentle face had changed. It was flushed and restless. She pulled out her hand from under the quilt and plucked at its edge with her fingers. Los kept taking her hand in his and tucking it under the quilt again.

"Open your eyes, dear, look at me."

She murmured plaintively, barely above a whisper, "Op win, op win." Her childish, barely audible, plaintive voice was trying to say, "Open the window." His feeling of pity was more terrible than fear. "Katya, Katya, look at me." He kissed her cheek, her forehead, her closed eyes. Her throat trembled, her chest rose convulsively, her fingers clutched the edge of the quilt. "Katya, Katya, what is it, my love?" No answer. She was going.... She lifted herself on her elbows, arched her chest, as though pushed by someone, tormented. Her head fell back. She slipped down, deep into the bed. Her jaw fell. Los, shaken, took her in his arms, clung to her.

No, no, no—he could not reconcile himself with Death.

Los rose from the cot, took a pack of cigarettes off the table, lit up and paced the dark shed. Then he climbed the steps to the telescope dais and trained the lens on Mars high over Petrograd. He gazed long at the bright, glowing little ball. It shimmered in the lens.

He lay down again. A new vision rose in his memory—Katya sitting in the grass on a mound. Away beyond the undulating fields shone the golden domes of Zvenigorod. Kites were gliding in the summer heat over the corn and buckwheat. Katya felt lazy, it was very hot. Sitting beside her, chewing a stalk of grass, Los gazed at her fair hair, her sun-tanned shoulders, and the strip of white between the tan of her skin and her dress. Her grey eyes were untroubled and beautiful. There were kites gliding in them too. She was eighteen. She sat there saying nothing. Los thought to himself, "Oh no, my dear, I have more important things to do than sit here and fall in love with you. I'm not going to get hooked. I shan't come out to the country to see you again."

Lord! How stupid he had been to have let those sultry summer days go to waste. If time could only have stopped in its pace then! But it was gone, never to return!...

Los got up, struck a match, lit a cigarette and began to pace the floor again. But striding up and down by the wall like a caged beast was worse still.

He opened the door and searched the sky for Mars, which had risen to its zenith.

"It'll be just as bad up there. I shan't escape from myself even beyond the Earth's limits and outside the bounds of Death. Why did I have to poison myself with love? Much better to have lived unaroused. Aren't the frozen seeds of life, the icy crystals floating in the ether, deep in slumber? But I, I had to fall and sprout—to learn the meaning of the awful thirst of love, of merging, of losing myself, of ceasing to be a solitary seed. And all this brief dream only to re-encounter death, and separation, and to float again, a frozen crystal."

Los lingered at the gate. High over sleeping Petrograd Mars glittered, now blood-red, now blue. "A new and fascinating world," Los thought, "a world long dead, perhaps, or fantastically lush and perfect. I'll stand there one night, just as I am standing here now, looking up at my native planet among the other stars. And I'll think of the mound, and the kites, and of Katya's grave. And my grief will no longer weigh me down."

In the early hours of the morning Los dug his head into his pillow and fell asleep. He was roused by the clatter of carts on the embankment. He rubbed his cheek. His eyes, sleep-laden, stared blankly at the maps on the walls and at the contours of the spaceship. He sighed, and fully awake now, went over to the wash-basin and doused his head in the icy water. Then he put on his coat and strode across the empty lot to his flat, where Katya had died six months before.

Here he washed and shaved, put on clean underwear and clothes, and checked the windows. They were fastened. The flat was not lived in. A layer of dust had settled on the furniture. He opened the door into the bedroom where he had not slept since Katya died. The shades were pulled down, and it was almost dark. Only the mirror on Katya's wardrobe door glimmered dimly. The door was half-open. Los frowned. He tiptoed over to it, closed it, then locked the bedroom door, walked out of the flat, locked the front door and put the key in his waistcoat pocket.

Now he was ready to leave.

THE SAME NIGHT

That same night Masha waited a long time for her husband. She heated the tea kettle on the primus stove over and over again, but the ominous silence outside the tall oaken door remained unbroken.

Gusev and Masha occupied a room in what was once a lavish mansion. Its owners had abandoned it during the Revolution. In the four years since, the rain and the blizzards had done a good deal of damage to it.

The room was big. On the ceiling, among the gilded ornaments and clouds, floated a plump smiling woman, with winged cherubs capering about her.

"See her, Masha?" Gusev was wont to say, pointing at the ceiling, "See that jolly lass? Plump she is, and has six babies. That's what I call a woman!"

Over the gilded bed with lion's paws hung a portrait of an old tight-lipped man in a powdered wig with a star on his coat. Gusev nicknamed him "General Boots." "He's the kind that never lets you off," he'd say. "Get on the wrong side of him, and he'll give you a taste of his boot." Masha was afraid to look at the portrait. A smoky pipe stretched across the room from a little iron stove, staining the walls with soot. The shelves and the table on which Masha cooked their frugal meals were very tidy.

The carved oaken door opened into a hall with a double row of windows. The broken panes were boarded up, and the ceiling had cracked in places. On gusty nights, the wind roamed in it freely, and mice scuttled across the floor.

Masha sat at the table. The primus stove sputtered. From afar the wind carried the mournful chimes of a clock. It struck two. There was no sign of Gusev.

"What does he want? What more does he need?" Masha thought. "Never satisfied, my restless darling. Alyosha, Alyosha, if you'd just shut your eyes and rest your head on my shoulder, sweetheart; no need to search, you'll never find anything like the love I have for you."

Tears glistened on her eyelashes. She wiped them unhurriedly and cupped her cheek in her hand. Overhead floated the jolly woman with her frolicking cherubs. Masha thought, "If I were like her, he'd never leave me."

Gusev had told her he was going away on a long trip, but had not said where, and she had been afraid to ask. She was aware that he could not go on living with her in the queer room, in that graveyard stillness, deprived of his former freedom. It was more than he could stand. He had nightmares—he would suddenly gnash his teeth, mutter, sit up, breathing hard, his face and chest dripping with sweat. Then he would go back to sleep, waking up next morning depressed and restless.

Masha was gentle with him—wiser than a mother. He loved her for it, but when morning came he would be anxious to be gone again.

Masha had a job, and brought home food rations. They often went without a kopek. Gusev picked up various jobs, but never kept them for long. "Old folks say there's a land of gold in China," he used to remark. "There's no such land there, of course, but I've never been out that way. I'll go there, Masha, and see what it's like."

Masha dreaded the moment when Gusev would leave her worse than death itself. She had nobody else in the world. She had been a sales-girl in the shops, and a cashier on the little Neva boats ever since she was fifteen. It had been a joyless and solitary existence.

A year ago, on a holiday, she had met Gusev in a park. He had said, "I see you're all alone. Mightn't we pass the time together? I hate being alone." She had looked at him closely. He had a nice face, kind eyes and a cheerful grin—and he was sober. "I don't mind," she had said, and they strolled in the park until night-fall, Gusev telling her about the war, raids and upheavals—things you would never find in books. He walked her home, and called on her often after that night. Masha gave herself to him simply, without fuss. And then she fell in love with him, suddenly, with every fibre of her being, feeling that he was very dear to her. That was when her anguish began.

The kettle boiled over. Masha took it off the stove and resumed her vigil. She had thought she heard a shuffling noise in the empty hall before, but had felt too forlorn and lonely to take notice of it. Now she heard it again. Someone was out there. She could hear his footsteps.

Masha flung the door open and looked into the hall. A number of low columns were faintly visible in the lamplight seeping in through one of the windows. Between them she saw a grey-haired old man, hatless, and wearing a long coat. He stood there glowering at her from under his knitted eyebrows, and craning his neck forward. Her knees buckled under her.

"What are you doing here?" she whispered.

The old man stared at her, his neck still craned forward. He raised a threatening forefinger. Masha slammed the door shut, her heart beating wildly, and listened intently to his receding steps. The old man was obviously leaving by way of the front stairs.

Soon she heard her husband's swift, vigorous stride approaching from the other end of the house. Gusev was cheerful and smudged with soot.

"Help me wash up," he said, unbuttoning his collar. "I'm leaving tomorrow! Is the kettle hot? That's fine." He washed his face, his muscular neck and his arms up to the elbows, looking at his wife out of the tail-end of his eye as he wiped himself. "Come, nothing's going to happen to me. I'll come back. If seven years of bullets and bayonets didn't get me down, my hour just isn't due—don't fret. And if I must give up the ghost, then it's in the books. Anything could finish me then, even a fly's tickle."

He sat down at the table, peeled a boiled potato, broke it in two and dipped it in salt.

"Get out some clean clothes—a couple of shirts, some underwear and foot-rags. Don't forget the soap. And a needle and thread. Been crying again?"

"I was frightened," said Masha, averting her face. "There's an old man snooping about in the house. He shook his finger at me. Please don't go away, Alyosha."

"D'you mean, because an old man's been shaking his finger at you?"

"It's an ill omen."

"Too bad I must go—I'd have it out with the old buzzard. It's probably one of the people who lived here, stealing about nights, trying to scare the living daylights out of us."

"Alyosha, will you come back to me?"

"Didn't I say so? When I say a thing, I mean it."

"Are you going very far?"

Gusev whistled and winked at the ceiling. His eyes danced as he poured hot tea into his saucer.

"Beyond the clouds, Masha, like the lassie up there."

Masha hung her head. Gusev yawned and began to undress. Masha cleared away the dishes noiselessly, and sat down to darn socks, scarcely daring to raise her eyes. When she took her things off and went to bed, Gusev was sound asleep, his hand resting on his chest. Masha lay down beside him and gazed at her husband. Tears coursed down her cheeks: she loved him so and yearned so for his restless heart. Where was he going? What was he after?

She rose at daybreak, brushed her husband's clothes and laid out the clean underwear. Gusev got out of bed. He drank his tea, joking and patting Masha's cheek. Then he put a big wad of money on the table, hoisted his sack over his shoulder, stood a moment in the doorway, kissed Masha, and was gone.

She never did find out from him where he was going.

THE TAKE-OFF

A little knot of gapers gathered on the lot outside Los's workshop. They straggled in from the embankment and the Petrovsky Island, jostling and looking up every now and then at the low-hanging sun pushing its broad rays through the clouds.

"What's up? Anybody murdered?" somebody asked.

"They're flying to Mars."

"Good Lord, what are we coming to?"

"What are you talking about? Who's flying?"

"They're going to seal a couple of convicts in a steel ball and shoot it off to Mars. It's an experiment."

"You're pulling my leg."

"The beasts—a man's nothing to them."

"Who do you mean by 'them,' may I ask?"

"None of your damned business."

"Inhuman, I call it."

"My God, what a pack of idiots you are."

"Who's an idiot?"

"They ought to send *you* up."

"Drop it, comrades. You're about to witness a signal event. Cut out your nonsense."

"But what's the idea of flying to Mars?"

"Well, somebody said they're taking up 400 kilograms of propaganda leaflets."

"It's an expedition."

"What for?"

"For gold."

"That's right—to replenish our gold reserves."

"How much do they expect to bring back?"

"Any amount."

"Citizens, how much longer do we have to wait here?"

"They're taking off at sundown."

The talk rippled back and forth until dusk. The people argued and quarrelled, but did not leave.

The setting sun shed a ruddy glow over half the sky. Presently a large car of the Gubernia Executive Committee nosed its way slowly through the crowd. Lights went on in the windows of the workshop. The people fell silent and pushed forward.

Open on all sides, its rows of rivets glinting, the egg-shaped spaceship stood on a slightly inclined cement platform in the middle of the shed. Its brightly-lit interior of rhomb-stitched yellow leather was visible through the open porthole.

Los and Gusev were clad in sheepskin jackets, felt boots and leather helmets. The members of the Executive Committee, academicians, engineers, and newspapermen surrounded the spaceship. The speechmaking was over. The photographers had taken ountless shots. Los said a tew words oı hanks. He was pale and glassy-eyed. He mbraced Khokhlov and Kuzmin. Glancing at is watch, he said:

"Time we took off."

A hush fell over the crowd. Gusev frowned nd crawled through the porthole. Inside, he at on a leather seat, adjusted his helmet and traightened his jacket.

"Don't forget to see my wife!" he called out o Khokhlov, scowling hard.

Los tarried at the porthole, looking down it his feet. Suddenly he raised his head, and said in a hollow, tremulous voice:

"I think I shall make it. I'm certain that n a few years hundreds of spaceships will ply the cosmos. We shall always—always be driven by the spirit of quest. But I should not be the first to fly. I should not be the first to probe the secrets of the firmament. What will I find there? Oblivion. It is this that troubles me most as I take my leave of you. No, comrades, I'm not a genius, not a brave man, not a dreamer. I'm a coward—a fugitive."

Los broke off abruptly, and looked oddly at the people around him. They were bewildered. He pulled his helmet down over his eyes.

"But that's beside the point. My personal affairs—I'm leaving them behind, on that lonely cot in the shed. Good-bye, comrades. Stand away from the spaceship, please."

Now Gusev called out from inside the cabin:

"Comrades, I'll pass the Soviet Republic's warmest regards to those whatever-they-are on Mars. Right?"

The crowd cheered.

Los turned, crawled through the porthole and slammed the lid shut behind him. Jostling and buzzing excitedly, the people pushed their way out of the shed and mixed with the crowd on the vacant lot. A voice called out warningly:

"Move back and lie down."

Thousands of people stared at the lighted squares of the workshop windows. All was quiet inside, and out in the open. Several minutes elapsed. Many lay down on the ground. A horse neighed in the distance. Somebody snarled:

"Silence!"

That instant the shed was shaken by an ear-splitting roar followed by a series of violent detonations. The earth shook. Out of the opening in the roof, in a cloud of smoke and dust, rose the blunt metallic nose of the spaceship. The roar grew as the craft bobbed up into the air, and hung there, as though taking aim. Then, with a thunderous din, the eight-metre sphere rocketed westward over the crowd and streaked into the reddish clouds in the distance.

The crowd came to life, shouting, throwing caps into the air, and swarming round the shed.

BLACK SKY

Los screwed the lid over the porthole, sat down, and looked into Gusev's eyes, which were as sharp and clawing as a captured bird's.

"Well, Alexei Ivanovich?"

"Let her go."

Los grasped the lever of the rheostat, and gave it a gentle tug. There was a dull detonation—the first crash that had startled the crowd on the lot. Then he pulled a second rheostat. A dull thudding started underfoot and the spaceship vibrated so violently that Gusev clutched at his seat and rolled his eyes wildly. Los switched on both rheostats. The spaceship shot up, the vibration subsided. Los yelled:

"We're up!"

Gusev mopped his face. It was getting hot. The speedometer indicated 50 metres per second. Its hand kept rising.

The spaceship was speeding at a tangent in a direction opposite to the rotation of the Earth. The centrifugal force was pulling it eastwards. According to Los's calculation, the ship would straighten out at an altitude of 100 kilometres and then move along a diagonal line.

The motor worked smoothly. Los and Gusev unbuttoned their fur-lined jackets and pushed back their helmets. They turned off the electric light and sat in the pale dusk filtering in through the peep-holes.

Fighting against a sensation of weakness and dizziness, Los got down on his knees and put his eye to the peep-hole. The Earth spread out below like a huge concave bowl of blue-grey. Here and there over it, like islands, lay cloudy ridges. He was looking at the Atlantic Ocean.

Gradually the bowl grew smaller and began to drop. Its right-hand edge took on a silvery sheen, and the other edge was lost in shadows. Now it looked like a ball hurtling into an abyss.

Gusev, whose eyes were glued to another peep-hole, said:

"So long, old thing. We've had a long spell together—time to part."

He tried to get up, lurched, and fell back into his seat.

"I'm choking, Mstislav Sergeyevich," he wheezed, tugging at his collar. "Can't breathe."

Los felt his heart beating faster and faster until it was pounding like mad. His head throbbed. Everything grew dark.

He crawled over to the speedometer. Its hand was moving rapidly, indicating an incredible velocity. The air was thinning. The gravitational pull declined. The compass showed that the Earth was directly beneath them. The ship was still picking up speed with each passing second, rocketing madly into icy space.

Los broke his finger-nails unbuttoning his collar. Then his heart stopped.

He had known that the ship's velocity would cause a pronounced change in the activity of the heart, in the blood circulation and the entire rhythm of the body. Knowing this, he had wired the speedometer of a gyroscope (of which there were two) to a tank which would eject a substantial dose of oxygen and ammonia at the crucial moment.

Los was the first to regain consciousness. His chest ached, his head reeled, and his heart hummed like a top. Thoughts came and went—unusual thoughts, quick and clear. His movements were light and precise.

He turned off the emergency oxygen taps and glanced at the speedometer. The spaceship was doing nearly 500 kilometres per second. A dazzling sunbeam came through one of the peep-holes and fell upon Gusev lying on his back, his teeth set in a horrible grin and his glassy eyes popping out of their sockets.

Los brought a pinch of smelling salts to his nose. Gusev took a deep breath. His eyelids fluttered. The engineer gripped him under the arm-pits and lifted him, but Gusev's body hung suspended in the air like a soap bubble. He released him, and Gusev sank slowly back to the floor. He landed with his legs outstretched and his elbows raised as if he were sitting in water. He looked about him in bewilderment.

"Am I drunk?" he gasped.

Los ordered him to climb to the top peep-hole and look out. Gusev struggled to his feet, staggered, then crawled like a fly up the sheer wall of the cabin, clutching at its stitched leather lining. He put his eye to the peep-hole.

"It's pitch dark," he reported. "I can't see a thing."

Los put a smoked eye-piece over the lens facing the sun. The sun hung suspended in space, a huge shaggy ball boldly outlined against the dark void around it. Two luminous veils of mist drifted on both sides of it like a pair of wings. A fountain spouted from the compact mass and shaped itself into a mushroom. It was a period of sun spots. A little apart from the radiant ball were iridescent oceans of fire. Cast off by the sun and revolving round it, they were paler than the zodiacal wings.

Los tore himself away from the fascinating spectacle—the life-giving fire of the universe. He replaced the lid on the eye-piece. It was dark again. Then he moved to the peep-hole on the other side of the cabin. He adjusted the focus. The greenish ray of a star pricked his eye, Presently a lucid blue beam replaced it. It was Sirius, the celestial diamond, the first star of the Northern sky.

Los crawled over to the third peep-hole. He adjusted it, put his eye to it, then wiped it with his handkerchief and put his eye to it again. His heart contracted. He felt the roots of his hair twitching.

Blurred, misty spots were floating past them in the dark.

"Something's out there next to us," cried Gusev in alarm.

The spots drifted downward, growing distinct and bright as they receded. Los glimpsed broken silver lines and threads, and then the boldly-etched jagged edges of a rocky ridge. The spaceship had evidently come near a celestial body, entered its gravitational field, and now begun to rotate round it like a satellite.

Los groped for the rheostat levers with a trembling hand, and pulled them as far as they would go at the risk of blowing up the ship. The engine under them shook and roared. The spots and shining jagged cliffs swiftly receded. The gleaming surface loomed larger, approaching them, and they could clearly discern sharp long shadows cast by e cliffs stretching blackly across a bare, eless plain.

The spaceship was heading for the rocks. ın-bathed on one side, they seemed to be stone's throw away. Los thought (his mind as clear and collected), "The ship will crash a moment, before it has time to turn neck remost to the pull of gravity. This is the ıd."

But just then he glimpsed the ruins of epped towers on the dead plain between the iffs. The ship slid over the toothy crags. eyond lay an abyss, a black void, obscuri- /. Metal-bearing veins glinted on the jagged ide of a steep cliff. Then the fragment of the mashed, unknown planet remained far be- ind, continuing its journey to eternity. The paceship was again speeding through the leserted expanse of black sky.

Suddenly Gusev started:

"Is that the moon ahead of us?"

He turned, parted from the wall, and hung n mid-air, arms and legs spread frogwise, :ursing under his breath, and straining to swim back to the wall. Los lost his hold on he floor, and felt himself drifting. He hung on to the ocular tube, and gazed at the glit- tering silvery disc of Mars.

THE DESCENT

The silvery disc of Mars, shrouded here and there in clouds, was growing perceptibly larger. The spot of ice at the South Pole sparkled dazzlingly. Beneath it spread a curve of mist, stretching to the equator in the east, ascending in the vicinity of the prime meridian, skirting a lighter surface, and bifurcating to form a second cape at the western edge of the disc.

Five clearly visible dark dots were distributed about the equator, joined by straight lines which formed two equilateral triangles and a third elongated one. At the foot of the eastern triangle was an arc. A second semicircle ran from the middle of this arc to its extremity. Several lines, dots and semi-circles were scattered to east and west of this equatorial group. The North Pole was immersed in darkness.

Los gazed avidly at this network of lines. Here it was—the thing that drove astronomers to distraction—the ever-changing rectilinear baffling Martian canals. Los now discerned a second, barely perceptible, blurred network of lines within the bold pattern of the first.

He sketched the lines in his notebook. Suddenly the Martian disc pitched violently, and floated past the lens. Los leaped to the rheostats.

"We're in, Alexei Ivanovich! We're being pulled in! We're falling!"

The ship turned neck foremost to the planet. Los cut down the motor, then switched it off. The change of velocity was not as painful now, but the silence that set in was so harrowing that Gusev clutched his head and pressed his hands over his ears.

Los lay on the floor watching the silvery disc grow larger and rounder. It seemed to be shooting towards them out of the void.

He switched on the rheostats. The spaceship vibrated, battling against the pull of the Martian field of gravitation. The velocity of their fall diminished. Mars shut out the sky, grew dimmer, its edges curving up like those of a bowl.

These last few moments were terrifying. They were dropping at a dizzy speed. Mars blotted out the sky. The lenses grew dim with moisture. The machine hurtled through a cloud-drift over a misty plain. Shuddering and roaring, it slowed down its descent.

"We're landing!" Los shouted, and switched off the motor. The next moment he was catapulted head over heels against the wall. The spaceship hit the ground heavily, and toppled on its side.

. . . .

Their knees trembled, their hands shook, and their hearts leaped wildly. Hastily and silently, Los and Gusev put the cabin in order, and stuck the half-dead mouse they had brought from the Earth out of one of the peep-holes. The mouse revived. It lifted its nose, twitched its whiskers, and washed itself. The air outside was fit for living beings.

They unscrewed the lid over the porthole. Los ran his tongue over his lips and said hollowly:

"We've made it, Alexei Ivanovich! Out we go!"

They pulled off their felt boots and fur-lined jackets. Gusev fastened his revolver to his belt (just in case), chuckled, and swung open the lid.

MARS

The first thing they saw as they crawled out of the spaceship was the dazzling bottomless sky, deep blue as the ocean in a storm.

The sun, a great fiery ball, stood high over Mars. The stream of crystal-blue light was cool and transparent—from the startlingly vivid horizon to the zenith.

"They've a jolly sun out here," said Gusev, and sneezed, so dazzlingly bright were the deep-blue heights. There was a tightening sensation in their chests and the blood throbbed in their temples, but breathing came easy. The air was thin and dry.

The spaceship lay in an orange-coloured flat plain. The horizon was very close—almost within reach. There were large cracks in the ground. The land was overgrown with tall cactuses shaped like pronged candlesticks, which cast vivid purple shadows on the ground. A dry wind was blowing.

Los and Gusev stood looking around for a while, then set off across the plain. They found walking unusually easy, although their feet sank ankle-deep in the crumbling soil. As they skirted a tall fleshy cactus, Los

ıched it. It quivered, as though swayed
a gust of wind, and its brown meaty ten-
:les stretched towards Los's hand. Gusev
:ked at its roots. The loathsome thing
ɔpled over, driving its thorns into the
ɪd.

They walked for about thirty minutes. Be-
·e them spread the same orange-coloured
ain—the cactuses, the purple shadows, and
: cracks in the soil. When they turned
ıth, leaving the sun at right angles to
:m, Los's attention was drawn to the soil.
ddenly he stopped short, squatted on
; haunches, and slapped his knee.

'Alexei Ivanovich, the soil's been
ɔughed."

"What?"

On looking closer they saw wide, crum-
ng grooves and straight rows of cactuses.
me steps away Gusev stumbled over a
ne slab with a large bronze ring. A shred
rope was tied to the ring. Los scratched
; chin. His eyes shone.

'Do you know where we are?" he asked.

'Yes—in a field."

'And what's the ring for?"

"The devil knows why they had to fix a ring in the stone."

"It's to fasten a buoy. See these cockle-shells? We're on the bottom of a dry canal."

"But," said Gusev, "they don't seem to have much water here."

They turned west and strode across the grooves. A large bird with a drooping asp-like body flew over the field, flapping its wings convulsively. Gusev stopped dead and reached for his revolver, but the bird soared, rose into the intense blue of the sky, and disappeared beyond the near horizon.

The cactuses were now taller, thicker and meatier. The men had to pick their way carefully through the quivering, thorny thicket. Animals very much like lizards, bright-orange, with scaly backs, scuttled underfoot. Strange prickly-looking balls scudded aside and leapt into the tentacled undergrowth. Los and Gusev proceeded with great care.

The cactuses terminated at the edge of a steep chalk-white bank. It was paved, apparently, with ancient hewn flagstones. Dry moss hung from the cracks and crevices. A ring like the one in the field was screwed into one of the slabs. Crested lizards lay dozing peacefully in the sun.

The space-travellers climbed the bank. On top, an undulating plain opened to their eyes. It was the same orange colour, but of a dimmer shade. There was a scattering of dwarfed trees, somewhat like mountain pines, and white mounds of stones, and ruins. Away in the north-west rose a mountain range, as sharp and jagged as frozen tongues of flame. The summits sparkled with snow.

"We'd better get back," said Gusev. "Have a bite to eat and rest up. We'll soon fag ourselves out this way. There's not a soul around."

They lingered on the bank for a while. The plain was heart-breakingly desolate and forlorn.

"What a place to come to," Gusev sighed.

They descended the bank and made for the spaceship. It took some time to find it among the cactuses.

Suddenly Gusev whispered:

"There it is!"

He whipped his revolver out with a trained hand.

"Hey!" he shouted. "Who's meddling with our ship, you blankety-blank? I'll shoot!"

"Who are you shouting at?"

"See the ship over there?"

"Yes, I can see it now."

"There's someone on its right."

They ran, stumbling, towards the spaceship. The creature near it moved away, hopped among the cactuses, leapt high, spread its long webby wings, shot into the air with a crackling noise, and, describing a circle over their heads, soared into the blue It was the creature they had taken for a bird. Gusev aimed his revolver at it, but Los knocked the gun out of his hand.

"You're mad!" he cried. "Can't you see it's a Martian?"

Gusev stared open-mouthed at the strange creature circling above them in the deep-blue sky. Los pulled out his handkerchief and waved.

"Take care," said Gusev. "He may plug us from up there."

"Put your revolver away, I tell you."

The large bird descended. Now they saw that it was a man-like being seated in the saddle of a flying-machine. Two curved mobile wings flapped on either side, at the level of his shoulders. A disc whirred a little below the wings—a propeller apparently. Behind the saddle hung a tail with levers protruding from it. The machine was as mobile and pliant as a living being.

It dived and glided over the field with one wing up and the other down. Finally, they saw the Martian's head in an egg-shaped helmet with a tall peak. He wore goggles, and his long face was brick-red, wizened and sharp-nosed. He opened his mouth and squeaked. Then he flapped his wings rapidly, landed, ran a few steps and jumped out of his saddle some thirty paces away from the travellers.

The Martian resembled a man of medium height. He was clad in a loose yellow jacket, and his spindle legs were bound tightly above the knees. He pointed angrily at the fallen cactuses, but when Los and Gusev made a step in his direction, he jumped back into his saddle, shook his long finger at them, took off almost without a run, then landed again, shouting in a thin, squeaking voice and pointing at the broken plants.

"The block's sore at us," said Gusev. "Hey!" he cried to the Martian, "stop squeaking, you old freak! Come on over here—we don't bite!"

"Don't shout at him, Alexei Ivanovich. He doesn't know Russian. Let's sit down, or he'll never come near us."

They squatted on the sun-baked ground. Los gestured that he wanted to eat and drink. Gusev lit a cigarette and spat. The Martian regarded them for a while, ceased his chatter but still shook his long, pencil-like finger at them. Then he unfastened a bag from the saddle and threw it to them. Next he re-mounted his machine, climbed in circles to a high altitude and flew off north, where he was soon lost behind the horizon.

The bag contained two metal boxes and a flat vessel filled with liquid. Gusev opened the boxes. There was a strong-smelling jelly in one and a few jellied lumps, much like Turkish Delight, in the other. Gusev sniffed them.

"Ugh, so that's what they eat!"

He fetched a basket of food from the spaceship, gathered a few dry cactus sticks and held a match to them. A thin wisp of smoke rose from the fire. The cactuses smouldered, but gave a great deal of heat. They warmed a tin of corned beef and laid their meal out on a clean napkin. They had not realized how ravenously hungry they were, and pitched in solidly.

The sun stood high. The wind had abated. It was hot. A small myriapod crawled up to them over the orange mounds. Gusev threw it a piece of crisped bread. Raising its triangular horny head, it froze into stony immobility.

Los asked for a cigarette and lay down, propping his cheek on his hand. He smoked and smiled.

"D'you know how long we've gone without food, Alexei Ivanovich?"

"Since yesterday, Mstislav Sergeyevich. I filled up with potatoes just before the takeoff."

"No, my dear friend, we haven't eaten for 23 or 24 days."

"What?!"

"It was August 18 in Petrograd yesterday. Today it is September 11. Surprised?"

"Surprised is not the word for it."

"I find it hard to understand myself. We took off at 7 p.m. It is 2 p.m. now. By my watch we left the Earth 19 hours ago. But if we take the clock in my workshop, it is almost a month. Did you ever notice how queer you feel if you wake up in a train when it stops or what an odd sensation you have if you sleep through the stop? Your body loses speed when the train stops moving. In a running train, your heart and watch both go faster than in a stationary train. True, you can hardly tell the difference, because the train's velocity is so insignificant. But our flight is another matter. We flew half the way almost at the velocity of light—and felt it only too well. As long as we were flying, our heart activity and every other motion were related, and were, so to speak, part and parcel of the ship's progress. Everything moved in the same rhythm. The ship's speed was 500,000 times the normal speed of a body in motion on Earth. Hence, the speed of my heart-beats—a beat per second by the ship's watch—increased 500,000 times. This means that by the Petrograd clock my heart beat 500,000 times a second during the flight. According to my heart-beats and the ship's watch, and the way I feel, we were en route 19 hours. And so we really were—just 19 hours. But if we take the heart-beats of someone in Petrograd, and the Petropavlovsky Church clock, more than three weeks have passed since we left the Earth. Perhaps, some day, we'll build a large spaceship, stock it with a six-month supply of food, oxygen and ultralyddite, and invite a few cranks to go up in it. 'Tired of living in our century? Want to live a hundred years from now? Get into this box and rally your patience to stay in it for six months. You will be well recompensed—considering what you'll find on your return! You'll have been gone a hundred years.' We'll shoot them into space at the speed of light. For six months they'll languish there, grow beards, then come back to Earth to find a Golden Age. That's what it'll be like."

Gusev said "oh," and "ah," and clicked his tongue in amazement.

"What d'you think of this stuff?" he asked. "Will it do us any harm?"

He pulled the stopper in the Martian flask with his teeth, tasted the liquid and spat. It was drinkable. He took a few gulps and smacked his lips.

"It's something like our Madeira."

Los took a sip. The liquid was sirupy and sweet, and held the fragrance of flowers. Before they knew it half the flask was gone. A pleasant sense of ease and warmth coursed through their veins, but their minds were unclouded.

Los got to his feet and stretched himself. He felt marvellously and strangely at ease under this alien sky, as in a dream. It was as though he were cast ashore by the surf of the stellar ocean—reborn to explore an unknown, new life.

Gusev stowed away the food basket in the ship, screwed the lid down on the porthole and pushed his cap back.

"I'm not a bit sorry I came, Mstislav Sergeyevich. I feel wonderful."

They decided to return to the bank and scour the hilly plain until dark.

In the highest of spirits they made their way among the cactuses, clearing them now and then with long, bouncy leaps. Soon they glimpsed the flagstones gleaming white through the thickets.

Suddenly Los stopped. His skin crept with loathing. Staring up at him from behind meaty cactus leaves some three paces away was a pair of eyes, as large as those of a horse, with drooping red eyelids. There was intense, deadly hatred in their piercing glare.

"What's the matter?" Gusev asked. Then he saw them too. He fired his revolver at once. There was a spurt of dust, and the eyes disappeared. "There's another!" Gusev turned and fired at a striped brown fat body moving swiftly on long, spidery legs. It was the kind of giant spider that is to be found on Earth on the bottom of deep oceans. It escaped into the thickets.

THE DESERTED HOUSE

From the canal bank to the nearest copse Los and Gusev walked in brown-baked dust, clearing dry ditches, and shirting ponds. Here and there, the rusty skeletons of what used to be barges jutted out of the sand of the abandoned canal beds. Convex discs a metre in diameter gleamed in the dead, dismal plain. They stretched in a line of glimmering dots from the craggy mountains down to the thickets and ruins below.

A clump of stunted brown trees with spreading flat crowns and gnarled branches nestled between two hills. Their foliage was moss-like, their trunks knotted and veined. Shreds of barbed netting were stretched between the outermost trees.

They entered the copse. Gusev stooped and kicked something in the dust. A fractured human skull rolled out. Metal gleamed in its teeth. It was hot there. The mossy branches offered meagre shelter from the blazing rays of the sun. A few steps away they stumbled upon one of the convex discs; it was attached to the edge of a round metal well. Then, at the back of the copse, they came upon the ruins of a thick brick wall. Mounds of rubble and twisted metal beams lay around it.

"These houses were blown up," Gusev observed. "They've been fighting. I've seen plenty of this sort of thing before."

A giant spider appeared from behind a heap of rubble and ran along the jagged edge of a wall. Gusev fired. The spider leaped high and toppled over. Another came running out of the ruins and made for the trees, raising little clouds of brown dust. It ran into the barbed netting and struggled vainly to extricate itself.

Gusev and Los came to a hill-top and descended in the direction of another little copse, in which they glimpsed a few brick structures around a tall flat-roofed stone building. There were several discs between the hill and the buildings. Pointing at them, Los said:

"They're probably the wells of a water main, complete with pneumatic piping and electric wiring. Seems they've been out of use for years."

They cleared the barbed netting, crossed the copse, and approached a sprawling flagged courtyard. At its far end stood a house of unique, sombre architecture. Its smooth walls tapered towards a massive cornice of black and red stone. The windows, set deep in the walls, were long and narrow as crevices. Two corrugated tapering pillars supported a portal with a bronze bas-relief depicting a reclining figure with closed eyes. Flat steps running the length of the façade led up to a low massive door. Wilted fibres of creeping plants hung between the dark slabs of the wall. The building resembled a huge tomb.

Gusev put his shoulder to the metal door and heaved. It gave way with a creak. They passed a dark vestibule and entered a large hall. Light filtered in through a glass dome. The hall was almost empty. There were a few upturned stools and a low table covered with a dusty black cloth. The stone floor was littered with broken crockery, and a strange kind of machine or instrument made of discs, globes and metal netting stood near the door. Everything was coated with dust.

Dusty shafts of light fell on the yellowish gold-specked walls, which were fringed with a wide strip of mosaic, depicting, apparently historical episodes—battles between yellow-skinned and red-skinned creatures; a man-like figure immersed up to the waist in the sea; the same figure flying amid the stars; battle scenes and scenes of combat with beasts of prey; herds of strange-looking animals driven by shepherds; scenes of domestic life; hunting scenes; dances; birth and death rituals. The dismal mosaic terminated over the doorway in a picture of a giant circular reservoir.

"Most interesting," said Los, stepping on to a couch for a closer look at the mosaic. "A strange human head keeps recurring in all the scenes. What can it mean?"

In the meantime, Gusev discovered a door which opened on to an inner stairway. It led to a broad arched passage flooded with dust-laden light.

All along the walls and in the niches stood stone and bronze figures, busts, heads, masks, fragments of vases. Marble and bronze doorways led to private chambers.

Gusev decided to investigate the low-ceilinged, musty and dimly-lit rooms. In one of them he found an empty swimming pool, on the bottom of which lay a dead spider. In another a smashed mirror ran the length and breadth of one of the walls. On the floor lay a pile of rotting rags and upturned furniture; in the closets hung decayed remnants of various garments.

In the third room a wide couch stood upon a dais under a skylight. The skeleton of a Martian hung from the couch to the floor. The place bore traces of fierce fighting. A second skeleton lay huddled in a corner.

Amid the rubbish Gusev found several coined metal objects, much like women's ornaments, and little vessels of coloured stone. From among the rotting tatters that were once the garments of one of the skeletons, he picked up two large dark-gold stones joined by a miniature chain. The stones glowed warmly.

"They'll come in handy," Gusev muttered to himself. "I'll give them to Masha."

Los stopped to examine the sculptures in the passage. Among the sharp-nosed Martian heads, statues of sea monsters, painted masks, and vases, whose shapes and ornaments were curiously like those of the Etruscan amphoras, his eye picked out a large statue of a naked woman with tousled hair and a savage assymetrical face. Her breasts were pointed and far apart. She wore a golden tiara of stars, which formed a thin parabola on her forehead. It was inlaid with two little balls—one ruby-red, and the other brick-red. The sensuous haughty face was strangely familiar.

Beside the statue was a dark niche fenced off with a netted screen. Los dug his fingers through the netting, but it would not give way. He lit a match and peered in. A golden mask lay on the remnants of a cushion. It was the mask of a human face with high cheek-bones and serenely closed eyes. The crescent-shaped mouth was smiling. The nose was pointed, like a bird's beak. A swelling between the eyebrows had the shape of a large dragon-fly's eye. It was the head he had seen on the mosaic strip in the first hall.

Los burned half his matches examining the curious mask. Shortly before his departure from the Earth, he had seen photographs of similar masks, discovered among ruins of giant cities on the Niger, in the part of

Africa where signs of an extinct culture suggested a race mysteriously vanished.

One of the side doors in the passage was ajar. Los entered a long high-ceilinged room with a gallery and latticed balustrade. Below the gallery, and on it, were bookcases and shelves with fat volumes. Their backs, stamped in gold, lined the grey walls. There were small metal cylinders in some of the bookcases, and leather- or wood-bound volumes. From the bookcases, shelves, and the dark corners blindly stared busts of wizened, bald-headed Martian scientists. Several deep seats and cabinets on spindle legs with round screens attached to their sides stood about the room.

Los surveyed this mildewed treasure-house with bated breath. Its books contained the wisdom of centuries. He approached a shelf and carefully pulled out a book. Its pages were greenish, and the letters shaped like geometric figures coloured a light-brown hue. He put one of the books with technical drawings into his pocket, to study it closer at his leisure. The metal receptacles contained yellow cylinders resembling phonograph records of old. At the scratch of a finger-nail they sounded like bone, but their surface was as smooth as glass. He saw one of them on the top of a screened cabinet. Someone had apparently been about to use it when the house was attacked.

He next opened a black bookcase, pulled out one of the leather-bound worm-eaten books, and brushed off the dust carefully with his sleeve. Its yellowed time-worn pages formed a long vertical sheet that folded like a fan. The pages, merging one into the other, were covered with coloured triangles the size of a finger-nail, running from left to right and back again, dropping and intermingling in irregular lines. They varied in pattern and colour. A few pages lower the triangles were interspersed with coloured circles of different forms and hues, combining to form diverse patterns. The interwoven opalescent changing forms of these triangles, circles, squares and figures ran on from page to page. Presently Los heard a barely audible, exquisite melody.

He closed the book and leaned against the book-shelves dreamily, shaken and thrilled by this new sensation. It was a singing book.

"Mstislav Sergeyevich!" Gusev called to him, his voice rumbling hollowly through the empty building. "Come here, quick!"

Los went out into the passage. He saw Gusev in a doorway at its far end, with a frightened smile on his lips.

"See what they have here."

He led Los into a narrow semi-dark room. A large square milky mirror was mounted on the far wall, with a few stools and arm-chairs before it.

"See this little knob hanging on the cord? I thought it was gold and tried to tear it off. Look what happened."

Gusev pulled the knob. The mirror lit up and on its surface appeared the stepped contours of big buildings, window-panes sparkling in the setting sun, and flapping banners. The muted roar of a crowd filled the room. A winged shadow slipped across the mirror, blotting out the city. Suddenly the screen flashed brightly. There followed a crackling under the flooring, and the mirror faded.

"That was a short circuit," said Gusev. "We'd better push on. It's getting late."

THE SUNSET

Spreading its narrow wings of mist, the flaming sun sank lower and lower.

The two men hastened back across the plain which now, in the waning light, looked even more desolate and wild than ever. The sun set rapidly behind the near edge of the fields, and disappeared, leaving a brilliant red halo in its wake. Its pointed rays lit up half the horizon, then turned ashen-grey, and died. The sky acquired an opaque quality.

A large red star loomed low over Mars in the glow of the ashen sunset. It gleamed like an angry eye. For a moment it filled the darkness with its smouldering rays.

Presently the lofty celestial dome came alight with stars—glittering constellations whose icy rays hurt the eye. The glowering red star burned brighter as it climbed.

When they came to the canal bank, Los stopped and said, pointing at it:

"That's the Earth."

Gusev pulled off his cap and wiped the sweat from his brow. Throwing his head far back, he gazed at his native planet afloat among the constellations. His face was sad and drawn.

"The Earth," he echoed.

They stood for some time on the bank of the ancient canal overlooking the plain and the blurred contours of the cactuses in the starlight.

Now a silver crescent, smaller than the moon's, appeared above the stark line of the horizon and rose over the cactus field. The palmated plants cast long shadows on the ground.

Gusev prodded Los with his elbow.

"See what's behind us."

Overhead, above the undulating plain, the thickets and ruins, shone Mars's second satellite. Its round yellowish globe, also smaller than the moon's, sank beyond the craggy mountain-tops. The metal discs on the mountain slopes shimmered in its light.

"What a night!" whispered Gusev. "Like a dream."

They made their way cautiously down the bank to the cactus field. A shadow scurried underfoot. A shaggy ball rolled along the reflections cast on the ground by the two moons. They heard something rattle. Then something squealed. It was a thin, piercing, blood-curdling sound. The glimmering cactus leaves stirred. Cobwebs, as resilient as nets, stuck to their faces.

Suddenly, the night was rent by an eerie howl. It broke off abruptly, emphasizing the deep silence. Shuddering with horror and loathing, Gusev and Los dashed across the plain, leaping high over the quivering plants.

At last they saw the steel casing of their spaceship gleaming in the light of the rising crescent. They ran up to it and sank to the ground by its side, panting heavily.

"You won't find me out in these spidery places after dark," said Gusev. He unscrewed the lid over the porthole and climbed into the ship.

Los tarried a little, listening and peering into the darkness. Suddenly he saw the fantastic, winged outline of an airship sailing among the stars.

LOS LOOKS AT THE EARTH

The shadow cast by the airship disappeared. Los climbed on to the wet casing of the machine, lit his pipe and gazed up at the stars. He shivered a little in the chilly air. Inside, Gusev fussed about, muttering under his breath as he examined and stowed away his finds. Then he stuck his head through the porthole.

"Say what you like, Mstislav Sergeyevich, these things are made of gold. The stones are priceless. I can just see my fool of a girl dance for joy when I show them to her."

He withdrew his head, and was soon still, the lucky chap.

As for Los, sleep did not come to him. He blinked at the stars and sucked the stem of his pipe musingly. How the deuce had those gold masks with the third dragon-fly eye found their way to Mars? And the mosaic? The giants drowning in the sea and darting among the stars? The sign of the parabola? Did the ruby ball symbolize the Earth? And was the brick ball Mars? Were they badges of power over the two worlds? It was unfathomable. The singing book, too, and the strange city that had appeared in the milky mirror? And why—why was the land so desolate and deserted?

Los knocked his pipe out against his heel. Would day never come? The Martian flyer they had met earlier in the day must have notified some populated place of their arrival. Perhaps the Martians were looking for them, and the recent airship had been sent to find them?

Los scanned the sky. The light of the reddish star—the Earth—was growing dim as it approached the zenith. Its ray struck at his heart.

He recalled the sleepless night when he had stood in the door of his shed on Earth and gazed up at rising Mars with the same chill grief. That was just two nights ago. No more than a day lay between this hour and that—on Earth.

Ah, Earth, so green, now immersed in clouds and now emerging luxuriant, rich in water, cruel to its children, yet loved by them....

His brain chilled. That reddish globe of the Earth was so much like a flaming heart. And man, an ephemerid, coming to life for a moment; he—Los—all alone had, with his mad will, cut himself adrift from it, and was now sitting like some forlorn demon on this wretched patch of desert land. So this was solitude. Was it what he had wanted? Had he succeeded in escaping from himself?...

Los shivered violently from the cold. He shoved his pipe in his pocket, climbed into the ship, and lay down beside the snoring Gusev. That simple soul had not betrayed his land.

Having flown across space and landed in ninth heaven, he was as much at home in it as he had been on Earth. He slept like a babe. His conscience was clear.

The warmth and fatigue lulled Los to sleep. Consolation finally came to him. He dreamt of the bank of a terrestrial river, birches rustling in the wind, clouds and sparkling sunbeams playing in the water, and a radiant white figure waving and calling to him from across the river.

Los and Gusev were roused by the loud whirr of propellers.

THE MARTIANS

Dazzling pink clouds drifted over the morning sky like skeins of yarn. Bathed in sunshine, a flying-ship was descending, now appearing in the deep-blue rents in the clouds, now vanishing behind the pink ridges. Its triple-mast frame with three tapering wings on each side looked like a giant beetle.

The silvery ship, moist and gleaming, pierced the clouds and hung over the cactuses. Vertical screws whirred at the tips of its short masts at either end, keeping the ship some distance above the ground. Step-ladders were lowered over its sides, and the flying-machine perched on them. Down the step-ladders filed the thin little figures of Martians. They were clad in egg-shaped helmets and loose silver jackets. Thick collars covered their necks and chins. Each was armed with a short automatic rifle, with a disc half-way up the barrel.

Gusev stood frowning near the spaceship. Clutching his Mauser, he watched the Martians line up in double file. The muzzles of their rifles lay across their bent arms.

"They hold their guns like women, the blighters," Gusev growled.

Los stood by, arms folded across his chest, smiling. The last Martian to leave the ship wore a black robe that fell in folds from his shoulders. His bare head was bald and knobby. The colour of his beardless long face was almost blue.

He plodded through the loamy soil past the double row of soldiers. His protuberant light-coloured eyes fixed upon Gusev in an icy stare. Then he turned his eyes upon Los. He approached the two men, raised his small hand in its broad sleeve and chirped in a thin, glassy voice:

"Taltsetl."

His eyes opened wider still and flashed with frigid excitement. He repeated the bird-like word and pointed imperiously to the sky. Los said:

"The Earth."

"The Earth," the Martian repeated with difficulty, knitting his brow. The lumps on his head turned purple. Gusev thrust forward a foot and coughed.

"We're from Soviet Russia—Russians," he rasped. "Come on a visit, see?" He touched his cap. "We won't hurt you." Then he turned to Los, "He doesn't understand a word I say."

The Martian's intelligent blue face was immobile, except for a red spot—a sign of mental strain—that spread between his eyebrows. Pointing gracefully at the sun, he enunciated a strange word:

"Soátsre."

Then he pointed at the soil and spread his arms as though embracing a globe:

"Tuma."

Next he pointed at one of the soldiers, who stood in a semi-circle behind him, then at Gusev, himself and Los, and said:

"Shokho."

He named a number of objects and heard them named in the language of the Earth. Approaching Los, he solemnly touched the engineer's forehead between the eyebrows with his fourth finger. Los nodded in greeting. When the Martian touched Gusev the same way, the latter pulled his cap over his eyes. "They treat us like savages."

The Martian approached the spaceship and gazed at it with suppressed amazement. Then, having apparently grasped its principle, he examined the huge soot-covered steel egg with great interest. Suddenly he raised his arms, turned to the soldiers, and spoke to them rapidly.

"Aieeoo," the soldiers wailed.

He placed his palm on his forehead, sighed, conquered his agitation, and turned to Los without a trace of his former reserve. His eyes, now dark and moist, fixed on the engineer.

"Aieeoo," he said, "aieeoo utara shokho, datsia Tuma ragheoh Taltsetl."

Covering his eye with his hand, he bowed, called a soldier, took a narrow blade from him, and scratched on the spaceship the outlines of an egg, a lid over it, and the figure of a soldier at its side. Glancing over the Martian's shoulder, Gusev said:

"He wants to put a tent up over the ship and station guards around it. But they might pinch our things. The lid has no lock on it."

"Nonsense, Alexei Ivanovich. Don't be a fool."

"But all our instruments and clothes are in it. By the look of that soldier over there—I wouldn't trust him within a mile of my house."

The Martian listened respectfully to their conversation. Los signalled his agreement. The Martian put a whistle to his thin-lipped mouth, and a shrill whistle replied from the flying-ship. The Martian followed this up with a series of signals. Thin wire antennas rose from the top of the ship's tall middle mast and emitted sparks.

The Martian invited Los and Gusev to board the flying-ship. The soldiers came nearer and surrounded them. Gusev glanced at them over his shoulder with a smirk, climbed into the spaceship, brought out two sacks of clothes, screwed down the porthole, pointed at it and tapped his Mauser. Then he shook his finger at the soldiers and scowled fiercely. They followed his movements with amazement.

"Well, Alexei Ivanovich, guests or prisoners, we've got no choice," Los said with a smile.

He swung his sack over his shoulder and the two of them approached the ship.

The vertical screws on the masts broke into a loud whirr. The wings went down, and the propellers roared. Guests or prisoners, Gusev and Los climbed the flimsy step-ladder.

BEYOND THE MOUNTAINS

The flying-ship headed north-east, flying low over Mars. Los and the bald-headed Martian remained on deck. Gusev joined the soldiers below.

He entered a brightly-lit straw-coloured cabin, dropped into a wicker arm-chair and contemplated the sharp-nosed short soldiers, who blinked their reddish eyes like birds. Then he pulled out his precious tin cigarette-case (he had never parted with it in all his seven years of fighting), tapped its lid, so much as if to say, "How about a smoke, comrades," and offered the soldiers cigarettes.

The Martians shook their heads in fright. One of them risked taking a cigarette. He examined it, sniffed it and put it away in his trouser pocket. When Gusev lit his, they backed away from him, whispering timidly:

"Shokho tao tavra, shokho-om."

Horror was written over their pointed reddish faces as they watched the "shokho" swallow smoke. But soon they clustered round him again.

Unabashed by his ignorance of the Martian tongue, Gusev told his new friends about Russia, the war, the Revolution and his own exploits.

"Gusev—that's me. It's from goose—a kind of big bird that we have on Earth. You've never seen anything like them, I suppose. My name is Alexei. I was in command of more than a regiment—a complete cavalry squadron, as a matter of fact. A hero, I am—one hell of a brave chap. What I do is pull out my sabre—machine-gun or no machine-gun—and chop 'em to bits. 'Hands up and surrender, you bastards!' is what I say. I'm chopped up a bit myself, but never give it a thought. Our military academy has a special course called 'Gusev's Sabre Tactics.' Believe it or not! I was offered command of a corps," Gusev tilted his cap back and scratched his head, "but I refused. Fed up. Seven years of fighting is enough to make any man sick. Well, then Mstislav Sergeyevich here came along and begged me to fly with him. 'Alexei Ivanovich,' he says, 'please come with me—I can't possibly fly without you.' So here I am."

The Martians listened to him in amazement. One of them produced a flask with a brown liquid smelling of musk. Gusev dug into his sack and pulled out a pint of vodka. The Martians drank it and broke into an excited chatter. Gusev slapped them on the back and made a great deal of noise. Then he emptied his pockets of all sorts of odds and ends and offered to exchange them. Delighted, the Martians gave him articles of gold for his penknife, his pencil stub and curious cigarette-lighter made out of a blank cartridge.

Meanwhile, Los was leaning over the net railing of the flying-ship and gazing down at the desolate undulating plain receding below.

He recognized the house they had explored the day before. Wherever he turned his eyes were ruins, copses and the ribbons of dry canals.

Pointing to the desert below, Los conveyed his surprise at so much barren land. The Martian's bulging eyes suddenly grew angry. At a sign from him the flying-ship climbed higher, described an arc, and headed for the summits of the craggy mountains.

The sun rose high and the clouds disappeared. The propellers roared, the pliant wings creaked and shifted as the machine turned and climbed, and the vertical screws whirred. Los observed that there were no other sounds besides the whirring of the propellers and the whistling of the wind. The motors operated noiselessly. For that matter, there were no motors in sight. All Los could see were round boxes, resembling dynamo cases, revolving on the hub of each propeller, and two sparkling elliptical baskets of silvery wire topping the front and rear masts.

Los asked the Martian to name various objects, and wrote them down. Then he produced the book of technical drawings and asked his companion to pronounce the geometrical letters. The Martian looked at the book with surprise. His eyes froze again and his thin lips curled disdainfully. Deliberately, he took the book from Los's hands and dropped it overboard.

The rarefied air made breathing hard. Los's eyes watered. Noticing this, the Martian gave a sign to descend to a lower altitude. The ship was now flying over the blood-red crags. Their broad ridge zigzagged from south-east to north-west. The ship's shadow skimmed over the rocky precipices glittering with veins of ores and metals, the steep inclines overgrown with lichen, the misty abysses, and icy peaks and glaciers. The land was wild and desolate.

"Liziazira," said the Martian, indicating the mountains. He showed his small teeth, glinting with metal.

As he gazed down at the cliffs, which reminded him of the funereal landscape he had seen on the piece of dead planet, Los espied the overturned skeleton of a ship marooned on the rocks at the bottom of an abyss, and silvery metal debris scattered round it. Farther beyond the rocky ridge jutted the broken wing of another ship. On the right was a third wreck, speared by a granite peak. Everywhere were the remains of large wings, broken frames and jutting blades. It was obviously a battle-field; the demons themselves, it seemed, had been vanquished on these barren rocks.

Los stole a glance at his neighbour. The Martian was sitting beside him, clutching at his collar, and calmly surveying the sky. Flying towards them in formation were long-winged birds. They suddenly soared high, flashed their yellow wings in the deep blue of the sky and turned back. Following their descent, Los saw the black surface of a round lake cradled deep amid the rocks. Leafy bushes grew on its shores. The yellow birds alighted at the water's edge.

The lake suddenly began to ripple and boil, a fountain of water spurted up from its centre and dropped.

"Soám," said the Martian solemnly.

They were nearing the end of the mountain range. A canary-yellow plain with large sparkling lakes loomed in the north-west through the eddying translucent heat waves. The Martian pointed to the enchanting misty distance and said with a dreamy smile:

"Azora."

The flying-ship climbed again. The moist air caressed Los's face and hummed in his ears. Azora stretched in a broad shining plain below. Criss-crossed by rippling canals and carpeted with orange-coloured copses and jolly canary meadows, Azora, or Joy, was like the little spring meadows one dreams of as a child.

Wide metal barges plied up and down the canals. Little white houses with pretty garden paths were ranged along the banks. Los saw innumerable tiny figures of Martians. Some were taking off from their flat roofs and darting like bats across the canal to the copses beyond. Pools and sparkling streams glistened among the meadows. Azora was a lovely land indeed.

At the far end of the plain shimmered a vast expanse of water, into which emptied the winding canals. The air-ship flew in its direction, and at last Los made out a broad and straight canal. Its far bank was lost in mist, and its muddy yellow waters flowed indolently past a rocky incline.

They flew on for a long time. Finally, the end of the canal hove in sight. The smooth side of a wall rose out of the water, stretching both ways to the horizon. The wall loomed larger. Los could now discern huge slabs of stone, with shrubs and trees sprouting from their crevices. They were approaching a giant reservoir brimming with water. Here and there little foam-capped fountains played on its surface.

"Ro," said the Martian, raising his finger significantly.

Los pulled his notebook out of his pocket and found the sketch of lines and dots on the Martian disc he had made the day before. He showed the drawing to his neighbour and pointed to the reservoir below. The Martian scrutinized the drawing with a frown, then nodded excitedly and indicated one of the dots with the nail of his little finger.

Leaning over the rail, Los saw one curved and two straight canals stemming from the reservoir. So that was the secret: the round spots on the Martian disc were reservoirs, and the triangles and semi-circles were canals. But who had built these cyclopic walls? Los glanced at his companion. The Martian stuck out his underlip and raised his hands to the sky:

"Tao hatskha ro khamagatsitl."

The ship was now passing over a scorched plain. A fourth, very broad dry canal cut a pink-red gash in it; its bed was planted with neat rows of vegetation. This was obviously one of the lines in the second network of canals that showed in a blurred pattern on the Martian disc.

The plain gradually terminated in undulating hills beyond which rose the bluish outlines of latticed towers. Wire antennas sprouted over their central mast again and began to spark. More and more latticed towers and buildings appeared behind the hills. A gigantic city emerged at last out of the sunny haze in a pattern of silvery shadows.

The Martian said:

"Soatsera."

SOATSERA

The light-blue contours of Soatsera, its stepped line of flat roofs, latticed walls covered with green vines, the oval mirrors of its ponds, and the transparent towers rising beyond the hills spread over a large area all the way to the misty horizon. A multitude of black dots came swarming across the city to meet the flying-ship.

The planted canal bed receded to the north. East of the city lay an empty gutted field strewn with mounds of rubble. At one end of this desert towered a giant statue, cracked and overgrown with lichen, casting a long dark shadow upon the ground.

It was the statue of a man standing with his feet planted together, and his arms pressed to his narrow hips. A stitched belt supported his mighty chest, and an ear-lapped helmet topped by a fish-tail comb glimmered on his head. The crescent mouth in his broad face was smiling, and his eyes were closed.

"Magatsitl," said the Martian, pointing to the sky.

In the distance behind the statue were the ruins of a big reservoir and the remains of an aqueduct. Looking down at them, Los realized that the mounds of rubble on the plain—the pits and hills—were all remains of an ancient town. The new city of Soatsera began beyond the sparkling lake, to the west of these ruins.

The black dots in the sky grew larger as they neared the ship. They were hundreds of Martians hurrying to meet the ship in their winged boats and saddles, canvas birds and parachute baskets.

The first to reach them was a shiny gold cigar of a ship with four dragon-fly wings. It swerved and hung over them. Flowers and coloured strips of paper came floating down to their deck, and excited faces hung over the rails above.

Los stood up. Holding on to a rope, he doffed his helmet. The wind ruffled his white hair. Gusev climbed out of the cabin and took his place at his side. Flowers showered down upon them in bunches from the boats above. The bluish faces, some swarthier, others a brick-red hue, registered excitement, delight and awe.

The slowly-moving flying-ship was now surrounded on all sides by hundreds of aircraft. A fat man in a striped cap waved his arms to them as his parachute basket swooped down in front. A knobby face peering into a telescope flashed by. A worried-looking sharp-nosed Martian with flying hair circled their ship in his winged saddle, aiming a revolving case at Los. Then a flower-bedecked basket flew past, carrying three pale large-eyed women in blue bonnets, flapping blue sleeves and gold-embroidered scarves.

The whirr of propellers and hum of the wind in the wings, the thin whistles, the glitter of gold, and the bright costumes in the blue air, the foliage in the parks below—purple, silver and canary-yellow—and the sparkling window-panes of the buildings were all like a dream. Los and Gusev were stunned. Gusev kept looking round dazedly, and whispering:

"Look at that, will you! Did you ever see anything like it!"

The ship sailed over hanging gardens, and landed smoothly on a large round square. The next moment hundreds of little boats, baskets and winged saddles poured from the sky, plopping on to the white flagstones of the square. The streets radiating from it were filled with milling crowds of Martians who were running, scattering flowers and bits of paper, and waving handkerchiefs.

The ship had landed beside a tall forbidding building of red-black stone, as massive as a pyramid. On its broad steps, between square tapering pillars that rose to two-thirds of the height of the building, stood a group of Martians. They were clad in black robes and round caps. As Los learned afterwards, they were the Council of Engineers—the supreme governing body of all the Martian countries.

Los's companion motioned to him to stay on board the flying-ship. The soldiers filed down the step-ladders and surrounded the ship, holding back the pressing crowds. Gusev gazed with delight at the eddying square, bright with gaily-coloured clothes, at the swarms of wings above, the piles of grey and black-red buildings, the transparent outlines of towers behind the roofs.

"What a city! Ah, what a city!" he kept repeating, stamping his feet in excitement.

The black-robed Martians on the steps made way for a tall, stoop-shouldered Martian, also dressed in black, with an elongated morose face, and a long narrow black beard. A gold comb, like the tail of a fish, trembled on the top of his round cap.

Half-way down the staircase he leaned on his stick and fixed his dark, sunken eyes on the newcomers from the Earth. Los also studied him appraisingly and guardedly.

"What's he staring at us for, the devil," Gusev whispered. He turned to the crowd and called out to them cheerfully:

"Hallo, Comrades Martians! We bring you greetings from the Soviet Republics. We've come to make friends with you!"

The crowd gasped in amazement, buzzed excitedly, and pressed forward. The grim-looking Martian clutched his beard and turned his lack-lustre eyes on the crowd milling in the square. The tumultuous ocean of heads gradually grew still under his gaze. He turned to his companions on the steps, said a few words to them, and pointed his staff at the flying-ship.

One of the Martians ran down to the ship and whispered a few rapid words to the bald-headed Martian leaning over the ship's side. The next moment whistles resounded in the ship, two soldiers climbed aboard, the propellers roared, and the flying-ship took off ponderously. Rising above the city, it set its course northward.

IN THE AZURE COPSE

Soatsera disappeared behind the hills. The ship was flying over a plain dotted here and there with monotonous lines of buildings, the pylons and wires of elevated roads, gaping mines, and loaded wherries moving up and down the canals.

Soon rocky pinnacles appeared among the patches of forest. The ship descended, crossed over a gorge and landed on a meadow sloping down towards a luxuriant dark copse.

Los and Gusev picked up their sacks and followed their bald-headed companion down the slope towards the copse.

A spray of water beating up from behind a tree sparkled iridescently above the glistening, moist curly grass. A herd of short-legged, long-haired, black and white animals was grazing on the slope. It was an idyllic scene. The water gurgled. A soft breeze blew.

The long-haired animals rose lazily to make

way for the men, and then padded off clumsily on their bear-like paws, turning their flat, gentle muzzles to look at the newcomers. Yellow birds alighted on the meadow and preened their feathers under the iridescent fountain.

The travellers entered the copse. Its weeping trees were azure-bluc. Their resinous leafage rustled on dry drooping branches. Away beyond the spotted trunks shimmered the waters of a lake. The spicy aromatic heat in the wood went to the men's heads.

The copse was cut by many pathways strewn with orange gravel. In the circular clearings, where the paths intersected, stood large statues, some broken and overgrown with lichen. Here and there, stumps of pillars and remnants of cyclopic walls reared above the vegetation.

The path they followed wound towards the lake, and soon they saw its dark-blue surface, and in it the reflections of the summit of a distant crag, and the gently stirring weeping trees. The gorgeous sun shone brightly. In a curve of the bank, on both sides of a moss-grown staircase leading down to the water's edge, were two great sitting statues, cracked and festooned with creeping vines.

A young woman in a yellow pointed cap appeared on the steps. She looked slim and youthful, blue-white against the massive background of the moss-grown sitting Magatsitl smiling eternally in his sleep. She slipped, caught hold of a rocky ledge and raised her head.

"Aelita," the Martian whispered, covering his eyes with his sleeve, and dragged Los and Gusev off the path into the copse. Soon they came to a broad clearing. In its grassy recesses stood a gloomy grey house with slanting walls. Arrow-straight pathways led from the star-shaped gravel ground in front of it across the meadow and down to a grove in which some squat stone buildings were scattered among the trees.

The bald-headed Martian whistled. A short chubby Martian in a striped robe came round the corner of the house. His dark-red face looked as though it were smeared with beet-juice. Squinting in the sun, he came towards them, but when he heard who the newcomers were, he made a move to flee. The bald-headed Martian spoke to him in a commanding voice, and he led them into the house, shaking with fright, looking at them over his shoulder, and showing his single yellow tooth.

REST

The terrestrian visitors were led to small, bright, almost bare rooms, whose narrow windows overlooked the garden. The walls of the dining-room and bedrooms were covered with white matting. Flowering bushes stood in pots in the corners. Gusev found the place comfortable: "Like a basket—very nice."

The fat man in the striped robe—the house steward—fussed and chattered, waddling from one door to another and mopping his head with a brown handkerchief. Every now and again he suddenly froze into immobility, stared at the guests with his sclerotic eyes and mumbled a few rapid words—a charm, most likely.

He filled the baths and took Los and Gusev each to his own bath, from whose bottom rose thick clouds of steam. The hot, bubbling, light water almost lulled Los to sleep. The steward pulled him out by the hand.

Weak from his bath, Los stumbled into the dining-room where the table was laden with vegetables, chopped meats, tiny eggs and fruit. The little crisp balls of bread, no bigger than nuts, melted in their mouths. There were no knives or forks, just miniature spoons stuck into each dish. The steward was struck dumb by the way the men from the Earth devoured his delicate food. Gusev was enjoying himself enormously. He found the wine with its bouquet of damp flowers especially good. It seemed to evaporate in his mouth and coursed warm and invigorating through his veins.

After showing the guests to their bedrooms, the house steward bustled about for some time, propping the pillows and tucking in the quilts. The "white giants" were soon fast asleep. Their snoring made the glass panes shake, the plants tremble in their pots, and the beds creak heavily under their un-Martian powerful bodies.

Los opened his eyes. Blue artificial light poured down from the skylight. It was warm and pleasant in bed. "Where am I?" he asked himself, but closed his eyes again ecstatically before furnishing the answer.

Radiant spots floated past—like dewdrops glistening on the azure foliage. A presentiment of joys to come—that the next instant something very wonderful would filter through those spots into his dream—filled him with a sweet unrest.

He smiled in his sleep, and frowned, trying to penetrate the thin haze of rippling sunbeams. But an even deeper slumber overtook him.

. . . .

Los sat up in bed. He sat still for some time, then got out of bed and pulled the curtains. Huge stars of an unfamiliar and strange pattern shone icily through the narrow window.

"Yes, yes," he murmured, "I'm not on Earth. An ice-bound desert and boundless space has brought me to a new world. Yes, of course, I'm dead. I left life behind."

He dug his nails into the skin over his heart.

"This is not life, nor death either. My brain, my body are alive, but I've left life behind."

He could not understand why for two nights now he had been yearning so much for the Earth, for himself who lived out there, beyond the stars. It was as though a living thread had been broken, and his spirit was choking in an icy, black void. He fell back on his pillow.

. . . .

"Who is it?"

Los jumped out of bed. The morning light poured in through the window. The little straw room was spotless. Outside the window, the leaves rustled and the birds chirped. Los passed his hand over his eyes and sighed.

Someone tapped gently on the door again. Los opened it. It was the striped fat man hugging to his stomach a large bunch of blue flowers sparkling with dewdrops.

"Aieeoo utara Aelita," he whispered, holding out the flowers.

THE BALL OF MIST

During their morning meal Gusev said: "This won't do. It wasn't worth flying all that way to land ourselves in this hole. Lolling about in a bath isn't what we came here for. They won't have us in the city—remember how that old beard glared at us? Beware of him, Mstislav Sergeyevich. They've kept us comfortable so far, but what'll they do next?"

'Don't rush to conclusions, Alexei Ivancvich," said Los, glancing at the bitter-sweet smelling azure flowers. "Let's bide our time. They'll see we're not dangerous, and will let us go to town."

"I don't know about you, but I didn't come here to waste time," Gusev declared.

"What do you think we should do?"

"I'm surprised at you. You aren't doped, by any chance?"

"Do you want to quarrel?"

"No, but we could have smelled all the flowers we wanted back on Earth. My idea is—since we're the first men to come here, Mars is ours—a Soviet planet. We've got to make that official."

"You're a funny fellow, Alexei Ivanovich."

"We'll see who's funny." Gusev tightened his leather belt, shrugged his shoulders and narrowed his eyes cunningly. "It's no easy job, of course, since we're all alone. But we've got to get a signed document from them stating they're willing to join the Russian Federative Republic. They won't give it to us without a fight, naturally—you saw for yourself that things are not so quiet here on Mars. I've a nose for this sort of thing."

"Do you intend to start a revolution?"

"Can't say. We'll see about it. What'll we go back to Petrograd with? A dry spider, eh? Nothing doing! When we get back we'll show 'em the slip of paper: here you are—Mars has joined the Federative Republics! Europe'll sit up and take notice! There's plenty of gold here for one thing—shiploads of it."

Los looked at Gusev thoughtfully. Was the man joking? His cunning guileless eyes were twinkling, but there was a little dare-devil glint in them.

Los shook his head. Touching the translucent waxen petals of the large flowers, he said thoughtfully:

"I never bothered to wonder why I was flying to Mars. I just flew to come here. There was a time when conquistadores set out in search of new lands. They steered their ships into the mouths of rivers, their captains doffed their wide-brimmed hats and named the land after themselves. Then they plundered it. Yes, I suppose you're right. It is not enough just to land—one must load the ships with treasures! We are to discover a new world, with its untold treasures! Wisdom—wisdom is what we must take back on our ship, Alexei Ivanovich."

"You and I don't see eye to eye," said Gusev. "You're a pretty difficult sort."

Los laughed.

"No, I'm difficult only for myself. You and I will manage quite well, my friend."

Somebody scratched at the door. His knees

bent with fear and awe, the house steward motioned the men to follow him. Los rose hastily and smoothed his white hair. Gusev gave the ends of his moustache an energetic twist. The guests went along a passage, then down a flight of stairs, and came to the other end of the house.

The manager tapped at a low door. A hasty, childish voice called from inside. Los and Gusev entered a long white chamber. Dust-specks danced in the shafts of light streaming down from the skylight to the mosaic floor, which reflected neat rows of books, bronze statues between flat bookcases, little tables on pointed legs, and the milky surfaces of screens.

A little way from the door stood a young ashen-haired woman in a black long-sleeved robe. Specks of dust shimmered in the ray slanting over her tall hairdress, and fell upon the golden book-backs on the shelves. It was the woman they had seen near the lake, the woman whom the Martian had called Aelita.

Los bowed low before her. Aelita fixed the enormous pupils of her ashen eyes upon him. Her white-blue elongated face quivered. The little nose and generous mouth were as tender as a child's. Her breast under the black, soft folds of her gown heaved as though she had been climbing a steep hill.

"Ellio utara gheoh," she murmured in a mellifluous, gentle voice, and bent her head so low that they glimpsed the nape of her neck.

Los could only snap his fingers in reply. With an effort he said in a strangely pompous tone:

"The travellers from the Earth greet you, Aelita."

He blushed. Gusev announced with dignity:

"Glad to meet you—Regimental Commander Gusev and Engineer Los. We've come to thank you for your hospitality."

On hearing human speech, Aelita raised her head. Her face was now composed. The pupils of her eyes contracted. She held out her hand palm upwards. Los and Gusev fancied they saw a little pale-green ball appear in it. Suddenly Aelita turned her hand and went past the book-shelves to the far end of the library. Her guests followed her.

Los observed that Aelita was no higher than his shoulder, that she was as gentle and ethereal as the bitter-sweet flowers she had sent him that morning. The hem of her loose robe brushed the smooth surface of the mosaic floor. She turned and smiled, but her eyes were still disturbed.

She pointed to a broad bench standing in a semi-circular niche. Los and Gusev sat down. Aelita took a seat opposite them at a reading table, placed her elbows on it and gave her guests an appraising glance.

They sat in silence a little while. A sense of calm and acute pleasure pervaded Los as he watched the lovely stranger. Gusev sighed and murmured:

"Nice girl—awfully nice, in fact."

Then Aelita spoke. It was as though she had touched the strings of a musical instrument. Her voice was beautiful. She repeated several words over and over, barely moving her lips. Her ashen eyelashes dropped and rose.

She stretched her hand out again. Los and Gusev saw the same little pale-green ball of mist, no bigger than an apple, nestling in her palm. It was all movement and opalescence inside.

Now both the guests and Aelita gazed intently at the cloudy, opalescent apple. Suddenly the movement in it ceased, and a number of dark spots appeared on its surface. Then, as he examined the spots, Los gasped: it was the Earth that was lying in Aelita's palm!

"Taltsetl," she said. pointing to it.

The ball revolved slowly. The outlines of America and the Pacific coast of Asia drifted past. Gusev grew excited.

"That's us—Russians," he said, pointing his finger at Siberia.

The ridges of the Urals and the ribbon of the Lower Volga floated past like a veil, and they made out the contours of the coast of the White Sea.

"Here," said Los, pointing to the Gulf of Finland.

Aelita raised her eyes in surprise. The ball came to a stop. Los tried to concentrate, and in his mind's eye he saw a section of a geographical map. Almost at once, as though it were a reflection of his imagination, there appeared on the surface of the little misty ball a black stain with threads of railway lines spreading from it in all directions, and the inscription "Petrograd."

Aelita studied the ball and then covered it with her hand—it now shone through her fingers. She glanced at Los and nodded.

"Oheo, kho suah," she said, and he understood: "Concentrate and try to remember."

He recalled the outlines of Petersburg—the granite embankment, the cold blue waters of the Neva, a boat diving in its waves, the arches of the Nikolayevsky Bridge in the fog, the thick smoke rising from the factory chimneys, the mists and clouds of sunset, a wet street, a sign over a small shop, an old droshky standing on the corner.

Aelita rested her chin on her hand and contemplated the ball. It reflected Los's memories, producing pictures which were now distinct, and now blurred. The dim gleaming dome of St. Isaac's Cathedral appeared, to be replaced by stone steps leading down to the water's edge, a semi-circular bench, and a fair-haired girl sitting on it in melancholy solitude—her face trembled and disappeared—and above it two sphinxes in tiaras. Columns of figures flashed by—a technical drawing, a spluttering forge, and sullen old Khokhlov fanning the coals.

Aelita gazed for a long time at the strange life passing before her in the misty ball. Presently the images became confused: pictures of a completely different nature invaded the ball—clouds of smoke, a fire, galloping horses, men running and falling. Then a bearded face dripping with blood blotted out everything else. Gusev heaved a long sigh. Aelita looked at him in alarm and turned her head. The ball disappeared.

Aelita sat for a few moments in silence, leaning her elbows on the table, shielding her eyes with her hand. Then she stood up, took a container from one of the shelves, pulled out a cylinder of bone and inserted it in a reading table equipped with a screen. She pulled a cord, drawing blue curtains over the top windows of the library, moved the table closer to the bench and turned a knob.

The screen lit up, and the figures of Martians, animals, houses, trees and various domestic utensils appeared on it.

Aelita named each object. The figures moved and converged, and she named verbs. Occasionally, coloured signs, like those in the singing book, appeared alongside the images, and there sounded an elusive musical phrase. Aelita then named a conception.

She spoke in a low voice. Unhurriedly, the objects of this strange primer drifted across the screen. In the still powder-blue darkness of the library, Aelita's ashen eyes gazed at

Los and her voice cast a commanding, but gentle, spell over him. He was in a daze.

Soon he felt that his brain was clearing, as though a misty veil had been lifted, and new words and conceptions were impressed on his memory. This continued for a long time. At last, Aelita touched her forehead, sighed, and switched off the screen. Los and Gusev were in a trance.

"You had better rest now," said Aelita in words whose sounds were still strange, but whose meaning reached the recesses of their mind.

ON THE STAIRS

Seven days elapsed.

Recalling them later, Los visualized them as a blue twilight, a wonderful calm in which he lived through a succession of glorious daydreams.

Each morning, Los and Gusev rose early. After a bath and a light breakfast they went to the library where they were greeted by Aelita's serious, gentle glance. The meaning of her words was almost clear to them now. There was a sense of ineffable peace in the twilight stillness of that chamber, and in Aelita's soft-spoken speech. Her moist eyes shone. They seemed to draw the two of them into a land of dreams. Shadows crept across the screen, and words effortlessly sank into their consciousness.

These words—only sounds at first, and then conceptions looming in a fog—gradually acquired meaning. When Los uttered the word Aelita, it stirred him in two ways; the first two letters AE, or "seen for the last time," made him feel sad, and the letters LITA, or "starlight," diffused a silvery radiance. In this way, the language of the new world fused itself as the finest matter with his consciousness.

The lessons went on for seven days. They took place in the morning, and after sundown until midnight. Finally, Aelita grew weary. On the eighth day they were not awakened, and slept until evening.

When Los rose from his bed he saw the long shadows cast by the trees outside his window. A bird chirped on a crystal-clear monotonous note. Los dressed quickly and went to the library, without waking Gusev. He knocked on its door, but received no reply.

Then he went outdoors—for the first time in seven days.

The clearing sloped down to the low buildings on the fringe of the copse. A herd of ungainly, long-haired khashi—something like a cross between a bear and cow—moved in that direction, lowing dismally. The setting sun shed its golden rays over the curly grass. The meadow gleamed like wet gold. Emerald cranes flapped over the lake. A snowy pinnacle washed by the glow of sunset loomed in the distance. It was a peaceful scene, tinged with the sadness of a day departing in golden tranquillity.

Los followed the path leading to the lake. He passed the same weeping azure trees on both sides, the same ruins beyond the spotted tree-trunks; he breathed the same cool air. But he felt he was seeing this lovely place for the first time. A shroud had fallen off his eyes and ears, for he now knew the names of things.

The lake glowed in flaming shreds through the foliage. But when Los approached the water's edge the sun had set and the fiery feathers of the sunset, its tongues of flame, spread midway across the sky in a golden conflagration. The fire died rapidly, the sky cleared, grew dark, and soon was spangled with stars.

The strange stellar pattern was reflected in the water. In the curve of the lake, on the two sides of the stairway, loomed the black silhouettes of the stone giants—watchmen of the centuries, sitting with their faces uplifted to the stars.

Los groped his way to the steps, blinded by the swift descent of twilight. He leaned against the foot of one of the statues and filled his lungs with the damp air and the acrid aroma of marsh plants. The reflections of the stars were blurred. A thin mist had risen over the water. But up in the sky the constellations shone ever brighter, and as his eyes grew accustomed to the dusk he soon discerned the sleeping branches, the glinting pebbles and the smiling face of the seated Magatsitl.

Los stood gazing into the night until his hand, which rested on the stone, grew numb. Then, as he moved away from the statue, he saw Aelita on the steps below. She was sitting there motionless, looking at the stars reflected in the black water.

"Aieeoo tu ira khaskhe, Aelita," said Los, listening with surprise to the strange sounds his lips were shaping. He spoke them with difficulty, as though his lips were frozen. His desire—may I be with you, Aelita?—had shaped itself of its own accord in these alien words.

She turned her head slowly and said:

"Yes."

Los sank on to the step beside her. Aelita's hair was gathered up under the black hood of her cape. He saw her face in the starlight, but not her eyes—only the deep shadows under them.

In a voice somewhat distant and contained she asked:

"Were you happy there—on Earth?"

Los took his time to reply. He scanned her face. It was motionless. Her mouth was set in a sad line.

"Yes," he replied. "Yes—I was happy."

"What is happiness like on your Earth?" Los peered into her face again.

"Happiness on our Earth, I believe, is in escaping from one's self. He is happy who is imbued with fulness and accord, and with the desire to live for those who provide this fulness, accord and joy."

Aelita turned to look at him. He saw her large eyes gazing in surprise at him, the white-haired giant.

"It comes from loving a woman," he added.

Aelita turned away. The pointed hood on her head trembled. Was she laughing? No. Crying then? No. Los fidgeted on the mossy step. Aelita asked with a catch in her voice:

"Why did you leave the Earth?"

"The woman I loved had died," said Los. "I did not have the courage to stay with my despair. Life was torture. I'm a runaway—a coward."

Aelita's hand crept out of her cape, touched Los's, and slipped back under the cape.

"I knew this would happen to me," she said pensively. "I had strange dreams when I was a little girl. I dreamed of tall green mountains. And radiant rivers unlike ours. And clouds—large white clouds—and rain, downpours of rain. And giant men. I thought I was going mad. Later, my teacher told me I had ashkheh—second vision. We, the descendants of the Magatsitls, retain the memory of another life—within us there is ashkheh, lying dormant like the seed that has failed to sprout. Ashkheh is a terrible force; it is wisdom incarnate. But I do not know what happiness is."

Aelita thrust both hands out of her cape and clapped them together like a child. Her hood trembled again.

"For many years now I have been coming to these steps to look at the stars. I know a great deal. I know things of which you must never know, nor need to know. But I was happy only as a child, when I dreamed of the clouds, the pouring rain, the green mountains, and the giants. My teacher told me I should perish." She turned again and smiled.

Aelita was so beautiful, so dangerous was the bitter-sweet aroma emanating from her cape and hood, her hands, face and breath, that Los was awed.

"My teacher said, 'Khao will destroy you.' *Khao* is descent."

Aelita turned away and pulled her hood over her eyes.

After a moment's silence, Los said:

"Aelita, tell me what you know."

"It is a secret," she said solemnly, "but you are a man, and I shall have to tell you a great deal."

She lifted her face. The constellations on both sides of the Milky Way glittered with frightening brightness, as if burnished by the wind of eternity. Aelita sighed.

"Listen," she said, "listen to me with calm and attention."

AELITA'S FIRST STORY

Twenty thousand years ago Tuma, or Mars, was populated by the Aols—the Orange Race. The wild Aol tribes—hunters and eaters of the giant spiders—dwelled in the equatorial forests and marshes. Only a few words have come down to us from those tribes. Other Aol tribes dwelled along the southern gulfs of the large continent where there are volcanic caves and salt- and fresh-water lakes. They were fishermen, and stored their catch underground, in the salt lakes. They took shelter from the winter's cold in the deep caves. There are still mounds of fish bones in them.

"A third group of Aols settled near the equator, in the foothills, near the geysers of drinking water. These knew the art of housebuilding. They bred long-haired khashi, warred against the spider-eaters, and worshipped the blood-red star of Taltsetl.

"An unusual shokho appeared among the tribes inhabiting the blessed land of Azora. He was the son of a shepherd and had grown up in the Liziazira Mountains. When he reached the age of seventeen he descended to the Azora foothills and went from town to town, speaking thus:

"'I had a dream. The sky opened and a star fell to the ground. I drove my khashi to where the star had fallen and I saw the Son of the Sky lying in the grass. He was very tall, and his face was as white as the snow on the mountain peaks. He raised his head and I saw light and madness flashing in his eyes. Struck by fear, I fell to the ground and lay prostrate for a long time. I heard the Son of the Sky take my staff and drive my khashi away. The ground shook under his feet. And I heard him say in a thunderous voice: "You shall die, for that is my wish." But I followed him, because I was loath to part with my khashi. I was afraid to go near him, for his eyes flashed with evil fire, and each time I prostrated myself on the ground to remain alive. Thus we walked for several days, leaving the mountains behind and driving deeper and deeper into the desert.

"'The Son of the Sky struck his staff against a stone, and water spurted from it. The khashi and I drank. Then the Son of the Sky said to me, "Be my slave." And I tended his khashi, and he threw me the remains of his food.'

"This was what the shepherd told the town-dwellers. And he also said:

"'The gentle birds and peaceful animals never know their dying hour. But the predatory ikhi spreads its wings over the crane, and the spider spins its web, and the eyes of the awful cha glow in the blue thickets. Beware! You have not swords sharp enough to slay Evil. You have not walls strong enough to shelter you from it. You have not legs long enough to flee from it. I see a sign blazing in the sky, and the evil Son of the Sky swooping down upon your dwellings. His eyes are like the red fire of Taltsetl.'

"The dwellers of peaceful Azora lifted their hands in horror as they heard the shepherd's words. And the shepherd said:

"'When the bloodthirsty cha glares at you from the thickets, become a shadow, and the nose of the cha will not smell your blood. When the ikhi swoops down from the pink clouds, become a shadow, and the eyes of the ikhi will search for you in the grass in vain. When, in the light of the two moons—ollo and litkha—the evil spider tsitli spins its web around your dwelling, become a shadow, and the tsitli will not catch you. Become a shadow, poor son of Tuma. Evil alone draws Evil. Avoid everything akin to Evil. Hide your imperfections under the thresholds of your dwellings. Go to the great geyser of Soam and bathe in its waters. And you will become invisible to the evil Son of the Sky—his blood-shot eye will pierce your shadow in vain.'

"The dwellers of Azora hearkened to the shepherd. Many followed him to the round lake, to the great geyser of Soam.

"But some demanded, 'How can we hide Evil under the thresholds of our dwellings?' Others grew angry and shouted, 'You are fooling us. The poor have sent you to put us off our guard and take possession of our dwellings.' Still others said, 'Let us throw the mad shepherd from the cliff into the hot lake; let him be a shadow himself.'

"Hearing this, the shepherd picked up his ulla, a wooden pipe with strings stretched across a triangle at its tip, and seated himself among the infuriated and perplexed, and played and sang for them. He played and sang so well that the birds ceased to chirp, the wind ceased to blow, the herds lay down on the ground, and the sun stopped in the sky. The listeners felt that they—all of them—had hidden their imperfections under the threshold of their dwellings.

"The shepherd taught his disciples for three years. In the summer of the fourth year, the spider-eaters came from their marshes and fell upon the dwellers of Azora. The shepherd went from town to town and said, 'Do not cross your thresholds. Beware of the Evil in yourselves. Beware of tainting your purity.' The town-dwellers listened to him. But there were some who did not wish to oppose the spider-eaters, and the savages slew them on the thresholds of their dwellings. Then the town elders got together, caught the shepherd, dragged him to the cliff and cast him into the lake.

"The shepherd's teachings had meanwhile spread far beyond Azora. Even the dwellers of the sea-caves carved his image in the cliffs. But it happened, too, that one or another tribal chieftain executed those who worshipped the shepherd, because his teachings were deemed insane and dangerous. The hour, however, arrived when his prophecy came true. In the chronicles of that day it is written:

" 'For forty days and forty nights the Sons of the Sky dropped upon Tuma. The star of

Taltsetl rose after dusk and glowed unusually bright, like an Evil Eye. Many of the Sons of the Sky dropped dead, many were shattered against the rocks and drowned in the southern ocean, but many reached the surface of Tuma and remained alive.'

"That is what the chronicles say about the great migration of Magatsitls—one of the tribes of the terrestrial race which perished in the flood twenty thousand years ago.

"The Magatsitls came in bronze egg-like machines that were propelled by the power released in the process of disintegration of matter. They kept leaving the Earth for forty days.

"Many of the giant eggs were lost in stellar space. Many crashed when landing on Mars. Some landed safely on the plains of the equatorial continent.

"The chronicles say:

" 'The Sons of the Sky climbed out of their eggs, tall and black-haired. They had flat yellow faces. Their bodies and knees were clad in bronze armour. They wore pointed combs on their helmets, and the helmets protruded over their faces. They held short swords in their left hand, and in the right, a scroll with formulas which brought about the end of the poor ignorant people of Tuma.'

"Such was the fierce and mighty tribe of Magatsitls. Their domain on Earth had been the City of One Hundred Golden Gates on the continent which sank to the bottom of the ocean.

"They climbed out of their bronze eggs, entered the towns of the Aols and took what they wished, killing all who dared to oppose them. They drove the herds of khashi to the plains and dug wells. They tilled the fields and sowed them to barley. But there was little water in the wells, and the barley-corn withered in the dry and barren soil. Then they bade the Aols to go to the plains and dig irrigation canals and build large water reservoirs.

"Some of the tribes obeyed them. Others said, 'We shall not obey them. Let us kill the newcomers.' Aol troops marched to the plain and spread over it like a storm-cloud.

"The newcomers were few in number, but they were strong as rocks, mighty as the ocean waves, fierce as the tempest. They crushed the troops of the Aols. The Aol towns were razed and the herds scattered. The fierce cha left their marshes and tore the children and women to pieces. The spiders spun their webs round the deserted dwellings. The corpse-eaters—the ikhi—battened to such an extent that they could fly no longer. It was the end of the world.

"Then the Aols remembered the prophecy: 'Become a shadow to Evil, poor son of Tuma, and the bloody eye of the Son of the Sky will pierce your shadow in vain.' Many Aols went to the great geyser of Soam. Many left for the hills, hoping to hear the purifying song of the ulla in the mist-laden gorges. They shared their belongings. They sought the Good in themselves and in others, and welcomed the Good with songs and tears of joy. Those who believed in the shepherd built a Holy Threshold in the Liziazira Mountains, and Evil lay hidden under it. Three rings of undying fire guarded the Threshold.

"The Aol troops perished. The spider-eaters were all slain in the forests. The fishermen became slaves. But the Magatsitls did not molest those who believed in the shepherd; they did not touch the Holy Threshold; they did not go near the Soam Geyser; they did not enter the mountain gorges where the mysterious song of the ulla was wafted by the wind at midday.

"Many bloody and sad years passed in this way.

"There were no women among the new comers—the conquerors were fated to die without leaving any descendants. And so a herald appeared in the hills where the Aols were in hiding. He was a Magatsitl of handsome visage. He wore no helmet and carried no sword. He had nought but a staff to which was tied a skein of wool. He approached the fires round the Holy Threshold and addressed the Aols who gathered thither from all the gorges.

" 'My head is bare, my breast is unshielded. Slay me if I speak an untruth. We are very mighty. We possessed the star of Taltsetl. We flew across the way of the stars called the Milky Way. We vanquished Tuma and destroyed the tribes who opposed us. We have built water reservoirs and great canals to collect water and irrigate the barren plains of Tuma. We shall build the great city of Soatsera, the City of the Sun, and we shall grant life to all who wish to live. But we have no women, and must die without fulfilling our predestination. Give us your virgins, and we shall father a mighty tribe which will populate the continents of Tuma. Come to us and help us build.'

"The herald put down his staff with the skein of wool beside the fire and sat facing the Threshold. His eyes were closed. And everybody saw that there was a third eye on his brow, with a film on it, as though it were inflamed.

"The Aols conferred and spoke among themselves, 'In the hills there is not enough food for the cattle, and little water, too. In winter we freeze in our caves. The gales blow our huts into the bottomless gorges. Let us do as the herald says and return to our former dwellings.'

"The Aols left the mountain gorges and returned to the plain of Azora, driving their herds of khashi before them. The Magatsitls took the virgins of the Aols and fathered the blue Mountain Tribe. And they began to build the sixteen giant reservoirs of Ro to collect the water that flowed down from the polar summits during the thaw. The barren plains were cut up by canals and irrigated.

"The new towns of the Aols rose upon the ashes of the old. The fields yielded rich harvests.

"Then the walls of Soatsera were built. The Magatsitls employed giant cranes which were operated by means of amazing mechanisms. Their knowledge enabled them to shift large stones and stimulate the growth of plants. They wrote their knowledge down in books with coloured spots and star-shaped figures.

"When the last man from the Earth died, Knowledge died with him. Only twenty thousand years later did we, the descendants of the Mountain Tribe, learned to decipher the mysterious books of the Atlantians."

A CHANCE DISCOVERY

At dusk, Gusev, who had nothing better to do, made a tour of the rooms. The big house was built to withstand the winter frosts. It had many passages, stairways, halls and a gallery—all immersed in an untenanted silence. Gusev wandered through the house, looked into all the corners, and yawned:

"They're well off, the devils, but it's a dull life."

He heard voices and the clatter of kitchen knives and crockery in the back regions of the house. The house steward was scolding someone in a stream of chirpy words. Gusev made his way to the kitchen. It was a low-vaulted chamber, in the back of which an oily flame could be seen dancing over some pots and pans. He stood in the doorway and sniffed. The steward and the cook fell silent, and backed away from him.

"It's smoky in here—smoky, understand?" Gusev said in Russian. "You ought to put a cowl over your stove. Barbarians—that's what you are, and you call yourselves Martians!"

Shrugging his shoulder, he went out on the back porch, sat down on the stone steps, pulled out his cigarette-case, and lit a fag.

At the far end of the meadow, where the copse began, a shepherd boy was running and shouting as he drove his lowing khashi into a brick shed. A woman with two pails of milk came up the grass-grown path leading from the shed. The wind ruffled her yellow blouse and the little tassle hanging from the funny cap on her bright-red hair. Midway up the path she put her pails down and waved away an insect, shielding her face with her elbow. The wind blew her skirt up. She squatted, laughing, then snatched up her pails and came running to the house. When she saw Gusev, she grinned, showing her small white teeth.

Gusev called her Ikhoshka, although she was really called Ikha. She was the steward's niece—a bouncing smoky-blue mischievous girl.

Dashing past Gusev, she crinkled her nose. He wanted to give her a playful spank, but restrained himself, puffed at his cigarette and waited.

He did not wait in vain, for Ikhoshka soon came back with a basket and a little knife. She sat down a little way from the Son of the Sky and pared her vegetables, blinking her thick eyelashes. He could see that she was a jolly girl.

"Why are you Martian girls blue?" he asked her in Russian. "Silly Ikhoshka, you don't know life at all, do you?"

Ikha replied, and, strangely enough, he understood what she said.

"At school we studied Sacred History and it said that the Sons of the Sky were very fierce. It looks like the books were wrong. You are not fierce at all."

"That's right, we're gentle as lambs," said Gusev, winking.

Ikha spluttered with laughter, and the peelings flew from under her knife.

"My uncle says you Sons of the Sky can slay a person with a glance. I haven't noticed it."

"Really? And what have you noticed?"

"Look here, answer me in our language," said Ikhoshka. "I don't understand yours."

"But I sound something awful when I speak yours."

"What was that?" Ikha put down her knife. She was convulsed with laughter. "I think you people on the Red Star are the same as us."

Gusev coughed and moved a little closer to her. Ikha picked up her basket and edged away. Gusev coughed and moved closer again.

"You'll wear your trousers thin if you keep sliding on the step."

Perhaps Ikha had put it some other way, but that was how Gusev understood it.

He was now sitting very close to her. Ikhoshka heaved a little sigh. She inclined her head and sighed again a little more deeply. Gusev looked round furtively and put his arm on her shoulders. She threw back her head and stared at him with wide-open eyes. Before she knew it, he had kissed her hard on the mouth. Ikha hugged her basket and knife to herself.

"So there, Ikhoshka!" said Gusev. She jumped to her feet and ran away.

Gusev plucked at his moustache and grinned. The sun had set and the stars were twinkling in the sky. A shaggy little animal crept up to the steps and gazed at Gusev with luminescent eyes. Gusev stirred—the animal hissed and disappeared like a shadow.

"We'll have to drop this nonsense," Gusev muttered. He pulled at his belt and entered the house. In the passage, Ikha suddenly appeared in front of him. He beckoned to her. Frowning from the effort, he told her in Martian:

"I'll marry you if needs be. You do what I tell you." (Ikha turned away and pouted at the wall. He gripped her hand.) "Here, don't start pouting now—I haven't married you yet. I, the Son of the Sky, haven't come here for nothing. I have important business to do on your planet. But I'm new here and don't know your ways. You've got to help me. Only don't you dare lie to me. Tell me, who is your master?"

"Our master?" Ikha said, trying hard to understand what Gusev was saying. "He's the ruler of all the countries of Tuma."

"You don't say!" Gusev stood still. "You're not lying, are you?" (He scratched behind his ear.) "What's his title? Is he a king, eh? What's his job?"

"His name is Tuscoob. He's Aelita's father. He's the head of the Supreme Council."

"Oh, I see."

Gusev took a few steps in silence.

"I saw a screen in that room over there. I'd like to have another look at it. Show me how it works."

They entered a narrow, semi-dark room furnished with low armachairs. A filmy mirror gleamed white on the wall. Gusev sank into an armchair near the screen. Ikha said.

"What would the Son of the Sky like to see?"

"Show me the city."

"It's too late. The factories and shops are closed, and there's nobody in the squares. Perhaps you would like to see our entertainments?"

"Let's have the entertainments."

Ikha inserted a plug into a socket in the switchboard, and, holding the end of a long cord, moved back to where the Son of the Sky was lolling in the chair, his legs outstretched.

"Here's a festival," she said, pulling the cord.

The hubbub of a thousand voices filled the room. The screen lit up and a view of arched glass roofs appeared on its surface. Great shafts of light were focussed on large banners, posters and clouds of fume of every colour. Below seethed an ocean of heads. Here and there, above and below, darted bat-like winged figures. Then the glass arches, the intersecting shafts of light and the milling crowds receded and were lost in a dusty haze.

"What are they doing?" Gusev shouted above the din.

"They are inhaling the precious fumes. Those clouds of smoke—they are the fumes of the khavra; they are very precious fumes—fumes of immortality, we call them. The khavra-smoker has wonderful dreams—dreams of living for ever. He sees and understands marvellous things. Many even hear the sounds of the ulla. Smoking khavra at home is punished by death. Permission to smoke it is issued by the Supreme Council.

In this house we are allowed to smoke khavra just twelve times a year."

"And what are the others doing?"

"They are guessing numbers at the lottery drums. Today everybody can guess a number, and the one who guesses the right one will never have to work again. The Supreme Council will give him a fine house, a field, ten khashi and a winged boat. It's wonderful to guess the right number."

Explaining all this to Gusev, Ikha sat down on the arm-rest of his chair. He put his hand round her waist. Ikha tried to wriggle out of his embrace, then gave up and sat still. Gusev exclaimed with surprise at the things he saw on the screen. "Well, did you ever! Now look at that!" Finally he asked Ikha to show him something else.

Ikha jumped off the armchair and fumbled with the switchboard. She could not get the plugs to fit the holes. When she returned to Gusev and settled back on the arm-rest, playing with the button on her cord, her face was a little dazed. Gusev looked up at her and grinned. Ikha was terrified.

"It's high time you married, my girl."

Ikhoshka looked away and sighed. Gusev stroked her back, as sensitive as a cat's.

"My sweet little girl, my pretty blue lass."

"Look at this, it's very interesting," she murmured weakly, pulling the cord.

A man's back blotted out half the screen. A frigid voice was heard speaking slowly. The back moved aside and Gusev saw part of a tall arch supported at the far end of the chamber by a square pillar. A section of the wall was covered with golden inscriptions and geometric figures. Below, sitting round a table with their heads bent low, were the Martians whom he had seen on his arrival on the steps of the gloomy building.

Aelita's father Tuscoob stood at the head of the brocade-covered table. As his thin lips moved his beard gently brushed the golden embroidery of his robe. He was otherwise rigid, as though wrought out of stone. His lack-lustre, sombre eyes were fixed straight in front of him, at the screen. Tuscoob was speaking, and though incomprehensible, his sharp words were terrifying. He repeated the word Taltsetl several times and struck the table with a scroll. A Martian sitting opposite him, with a broad pale face, suddenly sprang up. Flashing his white eyes at Tuscoob, he cried:

"Not they, but you!"

Ikhoshka started. She was facing the screen, but had neither seen nor heard anything while the large hand of the Son of the Sky had been stroking her back. But the shout of the Martian on the screen, and Gusev's repeated question: "What is it, what are they saying?" startled her and she stared open-mouthed at the screen. She gave a little gasp and pulled the cord.

The screen faded.

"I made a mistake. I connected the wrong. . . . No one dares to listen to the secrets of the Supreme Council." Ikhoshka's teeth were chattering. She clutched at her red hair and whispered in despair, "I made a mistake. It's not my fault. They'll send me to the caves—to the eternal snows."

"Now, now Ikhoshka, I won't tell anybody." Gusev drew her close and stroked her warm hair, as silken as an Angora cat's. Ikhoshka grew quiet and closed her eyes.

"Foolish little girl. What are you, a kitten? Silly little blue thing."

He scratched her gently behind the ear, certain that she was enjoying the sensation. Ikhoshka drew in her legs. Her eyes glowed like those of the animal he had seen at the back porch. Gusev felt a little frightened.

At that moment they heard Los and Aelita coming up the hall. Ikhoshka slid off the armchair and stumbled towards the door.

That night Gusev went to Los's bedroom.

"Something's brewing against us," he said. "I got a girl here to switch on the screen, and we listened in by accident to a session of the Supreme Council. I understood enough to know that we've got to be careful. They'll kill us, as sure as I stand here. It'll end badly for us."

Los did not hear him. He gazed dreamily at his companion, his arms folded behind his head.

"Witchcraft, Alexei Ivanovich. It's all witchcraft. Turn off the light."

Gusev stood still for a moment.

"All right," he muttered gloomily.

Then he went to bed.

AELITA'S MORNING

Aelita woke up early and lay in bed leaning on her elbow. Her broad couch, open on all sides, stood, as was the custom, on a dais in the middle of the bedroom. The dome-like ceiling terminated high up in a marble-framed skylight through which the morning light filtered into the room. The pale mosaic pattern on the wall was hidden in shadows. The shaft of light picked out only the snow-white sheets, the pillows and Aelita's ashen head resting on her hand.

She had spent the night badly. Confused snatches of strange and alarming dreams had passed before her closed eyes. Her sleep had been light. All night she had had the sensation of being asleep and dreaming of tiresome things, and wondering drowsily why she was dreaming at all.

When the morning sun shone down through the skylight, Aelita sighed, woke up altogether, and lay motionless. Her thoughts were clear, but there was still a sense of longing in her blood. This was deplorable, very deplorable.

"Longing in the blood, confusion in the mind—a futile return to the experiences of the past. Longing of the blood—a return to the caves, the herds, the camp-fires. The spring breeze, longing, and birth. To give birth, rear creatures that they should die, then bury them, and again—the longing and the anguish of motherhood. Futile, blind reproduction."

Thus Aelita mused. Her reflections were wise, but her sense of longing would not allay itself. She got out of bed, slipped her feet into her straw slippers, pulled on her robe and went to her bathroom. There she undressed, tied her hair in a tight knot, and stepped into the marble pool.

She halted on the lowest step. It was pleasant to stand there in the sunlight pouring through the window. Sunbeams played on the wall. Aelita saw her reflection in the bluish water; a shaft of light fell on her stomach. Her top lip trembled with aversion. She dipped herself in the cool waters of the pool.

The bath refreshed her, and her thoughts returned to the cares of the day. Every morning she spoke to her father. There was a little screen in her room for the purpose.

Aelita sat down at her mirror, combed her hair, and smeared aromatic cream and a floral essence over her face, neck and arms. Then, frowning at herself, she pulled up the little table with the screen and plugged in the cipher-board.

Her father's familiar study appeared in the misty screen, with its bookcases, maps and drawings on revolving prisms. Tuscoob entered the room, sat down at his desk, pushed some manuscripts aside with his elbow and fixed his eyes on Aelita's. Smiling with the corners of his long thin lips, he said:

"How did you sleep, Aelita?"

"I slept well. Everything is well in the house."

"How are the Sons of the Sky?"

"They are calm and contented—still asleep."

"Are you still giving them lessons?"

"No. The engineer speaks fluently. His companion knows enough."

"Are they anxious to leave the house?"

"No—oh, no."

Aelita had answered too hastily. Tuscoob's lack-lustre eyes widened in surprise. Under his gaze Aelita began to edge back in her chair until she could move no farther. Her father said:

"I do not understand."

"What don't you understand? Father, tell me everything. What do you want to do with them? I beg you. . . ."

Aelita did not finish. Tuscoob's face was a mask of fury. The screen faded, but Aelita still scanned its dim surface, still saw her father's face which she, as all living things, dreaded.

She was disturbed more than ever, and studied her reflection in the mirror with dilated pupils. A vague sense of longing coursed through her blood. "This is very bad, and so futile."

The visage of the Son of the Sky appeared before her just as she saw it in the dream she had had that night—big, with snow-white hair, agitated, inexplicably changeable, with eyes now sad, now tender, saturated with the Earth's sun, the Earth's moisture—eyes as dangerous as the misty abysses, eyes that were stirring and tempestuous.

Aelita shook her head. Her heart beat painfully. Bending over the switchboard, she inserted the plugs. The misty screen revealed the wizened figure of an old man dozing in a chair among a great number of cushions. The light from a small window fell on his withered hands lying on a fluffy rug. The old man started, adjusted his glasses, peered over them at the screen and smiled toothlessly.

"What is it, my child?"

"Teacher, I am disturbed," said Aelita. "I cannot think clearly. I do not wish it. I am afraid. But I cannot help it."

"Are you disturbed by the Son of the Sky?"

"Yes. I am disturbed by what I cannot understand in him. Teacher, I have just spoken with Father. He was troubled. I feel there is conflict in the Supreme Council. I am afraid they will make a terrible decision. Help me."

"You have just said that the Son of the Sky disturbed you. Would not it be better if he were to disappear altogether?"

"Oh, no!" Aelita said this hastily, abruptly, in great perturbation.

The old man frowned. He champed his shrivelled mouth.

"I find it hard to follow your way of thinking, Aelita. There is both reality and contradiction in it."

"Yes, I feel that."

"That is the best proof of guilt. Supreme thought is clear, dispassionate and direct. I shall do as you wish. I shall speak to your father. He is also a passionate man, and that may cause him to act in a way that is neither wise nor just."

"I shall hope."

"Calm yourself, Aelita, and concentrate. Look into yourself. What is your disturbance? It is ancient silt—the red dusk—rising from the bottom of your blood—it is the thirst to prolong life. Your blood is revolting."

"Teacher, he disturbs me in another way."

"No matter what lofty feelings he may rouse in you, the woman will awaken in you, and you will perish. The frigidity of wisdom alone, Aelita, calm contemplation of inevitable death—the death of matter steeped in sweat and lust—and the anticipation of the time when your spirit, perfect, no more in need of the paltry experience of life, quits the boundaries of your consciousness and is no more—that, and that alone, is happiness. You are anxious to return. Beware of the temptation, my child. It is easy to fall, but the climb is slow and hard. Be wise."

Aelita's head drooped.

"Teacher," she said suddenly, her lips trembling and her eyes full of yearning, "the Son of the Sky said that on Earth they know that which is higher than reason, than knowledge, than wisdom. But what it was I did not understand. It is this that disturbs me. Yesterday, we were on the lake. When the Red Star rose, he pointed to it and said, 'It is surrounded by a mist of love.

Men who have known love do not die.' My heart was rent with longing, teacher."

The old man frowned and said nothing. The fingers of his withered hand twitched. "Good," he said. "Let the Son of the Sky impart his knowledge to you. Do not disturb me until you know all. But be careful."

The screen faded. It was quiet in the room. Aelita wiped her face with a handkerchief. Then she looked at herself—carefully, appraisingly. Her brows lifted. She opened a small casket and leaned over it as she fingered the objects within. She found and put on her neck a tiny dry paw of the wonderful animal indri, set in a frame of precious metal. It was believed to help women in trouble.

Aelita sighed and went to the library. Los rose from his seat at the window where he had been reading a book. Aelita looked at him—he was big, kind and worried. A great warmth surged up in her heart. She placed her hand on her breast, on the paw of the wonderful little animal, and said:

"Yesterday I promised to tell you about the end of the Atlantians. Sit down and listen."

AELITA'S SECOND STORY

"This is what we read in the coloured books," Aelita began. "At that distant time the hub of the Earth was the City of a Hundred Golden Gates, which now lies at the bottom of the ocean. Knowledge and the enticements of luxury spread from it far and wide. It attracted the earthly tribes and fired them with primeval greed. But a time came when a younger generation fell upon the rulers and captured the city. The light of civilization waned. Then it flared up again, brighter than ever, enriched by the fresh blood of the conquerors. Centuries passed, and again hordes of nomads hovered like a cloud over the eternal city.

"The original founders of the City of a Hundred Golden Gates were African Negroes of the Zemze tribe. They deemed themselves to be the junior branch of a black race which in the dimmest antiquity populated the gigantic continent of Gwandan, now lying at the bottom of the Pacific Ocean. Its survivers had broken up into numerous tribes. Many of them had become savages. But the memory of their great past was treasured by the Negroes.

"The Zemze people were powerful and tall. They had an extraordinary quality: they sensed the nature and form of things at a distance, just as a magnet senses the presence of another magnet. This special sense of theirs developed when they lived in the dark caves of tropical forests.

"The poisonous gokh fly drove the Zemzes out of the forests. They moved west until they found suitable land and finally settled on a hilly plateau washed on two sides by big rivers. There was much fruit and game there, and gold, tin and copper in the mountains. The forests, hills and quiet rivers were beautiful, and there were no ravishing fevers.

"The men built a wall to protect themselves from wild beasts, and erected a tall stone pyramid to show that they had come to stay.

"On the top of the pyramid they mounted a pillar crowned with a bunch of feathers of the klitli, the patron bird of the tribe which had saved them from the gokh fly during their migration to the west. The Zemze chieftains decorated their heads with feathers and gave themselves the names of birds.

"West of this plateau lived nomadic red-skinned tribes. The Zemze people fell upon these tribes, captured them, and made them till the soil, build houses and mine ore and gold. Word of the city spread far and wide, and the red-skinned tribes were terrified, for the Zemzes were strong and clever, and knew how to kill their enemies from afar with the aid of bent pieces of wood. They plied the wide rivers in their canoes and gathered tribute from the red-skins.

"The descendants of the Zemzes decorated their city with round stone buildings roofed with reeds. They wove excellent cloths of wool and recorded their thoughts with the help of drawings—an art that had been stored in their memories since ancient times.

"Many centuries passed, and now a great chieftain appeared among the red-skins. He was called Uru. Born in the city, he left it in his youth to join the nomads and hunters of the steppe. He gathered warriors round him in great numbers and set out to storm the city.

"The descendants of the Zemzes employed all the knowledge at their disposal to defend their town. They made use of fire, let mad buffaloes loose on the enemy, shot their boomerangs at them. But the red-skins were numerically stronger. And they were driven on by greed. They captured the city and laid it waste. Uru proclaimed himself ruler of the world. He bade the red warriors to take the Zemze virgins. The remnants of the vanquished tribe, who had taken refuge in the forests, returned to the city to serve the conquerors.

"The red-skins now mastered the knowledge, customs and arts of the Zemzes. They produced a long line of statesmen and conquerors, and the mysterious aptitude of sensing the nature of things from a distance was passed down from generation to generation.

"The generals of the Uru dynasty enlarged their domains, exterminated the nomads in the west and built pyramids of earth and stone on the coast of the Pacific Ocean. They pushed the Negroes far back to the east, and erected formidable fortresses along the banks of the Niger and Congo, and on the rocky coast of the Mediterranean which once spread to where the Sahara Desert now lies. It was an era of war and construction. The land of the Zemzes was called Hamagan.

"A new wall was put up round the city. It had a hundred gates adorned with gold foil. The peoples of the whole world flocked thither, drawn by greed and curiosity. Among the numerous tribes wandering through its bazaars and pitching their tents under its walls there appeared a new race of men. Their skin was dark-olive, their eyes narrow and smouldering, and their noses hooked like beaks. They were clever and cunning. Nobody knew how they had entered the city. But by the time a new generation had grown up the science and trade of the City of a Hundred Golden Gates had passed into the hands of this small tribe. They called themselves Sons of Aam.

"The wisest of the Sons of Aam deciphered the ancient inscriptions of the Zemzes and trained themselves to perceive the nature of things. They built a subterranean temple dedicated to the Sleeping Negro's Head and gathered about themselves followers, healing the sick, telling fortunes and showing the Believers the shadows of the dead.

"Their wealth and knowledge helped the Sons of Aam to worm their way into the government of the country. They won many tribes over to their side and incited them to rise both within and far beyond the limits of the city in the name of the new faith. The Uru dynasty was overthrown. The Sons of Aam now ruled the city.

"This was the time of the first great earthquake. Flames broke out here and there in the mountains and veiled the heavens with ashes. Large areas in the south of the Atlantis continent were swallowed up by the ocean. In the north, rocky islands rose from the sea bottom and merged with the mainland to form the European plain.

"The Sons of Aam brought culture to the numerous tribes vanquished and banished by the Uru dynasty. They had no use for warfare, however. Instead, they fitted out ships bearing the emblem of the Sleeping Negro's Head, and loaded them with spices, fabrics, gold and ivory. Those initiated in the cult sailed the ships to distant lands in the guise of merchants and doctors. They traded, and healed the sick and the lame by means of charms and invocations. To protect their wares, they built large pyramidal buildings in each land and mounted their Sleeping Negro's Head upon them. Thus they propagated their cult. If the people protested against their invasions, troops of red-skins clad in bronze armour and tall helmets, and armed with shields decorated with feathers swarmed down from the ships and struck terror into the hearts of the natives.

"Thus the ancient Zemze country was extended and fortified. But now it was called Atlantis. A second great city—Ptitligua—was built in the far west, in the land of the red-skins. Atlantian merchants sailed east to India, where the black race still reigned. They came to the east coast of Asia, where giants with flat yellow faces hurled stones at their ships.

"The cult of the Sleeping Head was open to all—it was the chief instrument of power, but its idea and inner essence were kept a secret. The Atlantians cultivated the Zemze grain of wisdom, and were no more than at the source of the road that led the whole race to destruction.

"This is what they said:

" 'The true world cannot be seen, sensed or heard; it has neither taste nor smell. It is the movement of reason. The initial and final purpose of this movement is indefinable. Reason is matter harder than stone and swifter than light. In pursuit of peace, like all matter, reason falls into a state of torpor; its movement becomes sluggish. The effect is called reincarnation of reason in substance. At a certain stage of its torpor, reason turns into fire, air, water and earth. It is from these four elements that the perceptible world is formed. Substance is a temporary condensation of reason. It is a nucleus of the sphere of condensed reason, even as a ball of lightning, which is a concentration of storm-laden air.

"'In a crystal, reason is at a consummate standstill. In interstellar space it is in consummate movement. Man is the bridge spanning these two states of reason. It is through man that reason flows into the perceptible world. The feet of man stem from crystal. His stomach is the sun, his eyes—the stars, and his head—the bowl whose edges spread into the universe.

"'Man is the world's ruler. The elements and all movement are subordinate to him. He rules them by the force that emanates from his reason, just as a sunbeam emanates from a crack in a clay vessel.'

"This is what the Atlantians said. The simple people did not grasp their teachings. Some worshipped animals; others—the shadows of the dead; still others worshipped idols, or the night's whispers, or thunder and lightning, or just a hole in the ground. It was impossible and dangerous to combat these numerous superstitions.

"Then the priests, the highest caste of Atlantians, realized the need of a single cult, a clear and comprehensible cult for all. They built huge gold-embellished temples and dedicated them to the Sun—the father and ruler of all life, the wrathful life-giver who dies and comes to life again.

"The cult of the Sun soon spread throughout the Earth. The Believers shed much human blood. Among the red-skins in the far west the sun was represented as a snake covered with feathers. In the far east the sun—king of the shadows of the dead—was depicted as a human being with the head of a bird.

"In the heart of the world—the City of a Hundred Golden Gates—a pyramid was built to the very clouds, and the Sleeping Head was mounted on its pinnacle. A golden winged bull with a human face and a lion's paws was erected in the square at its foot, and an undying flame lit under it.

"During the equinox, the high priest—the Son of the Sun and Great Potentate—sacrificed the handsomest youth in the city and cremated his body in the bull's belly in the presence of the people, to the accompaniment of egg-shaped drums and the dancing of nude women.

"The Son of the Sun was the supreme sovereign of the city and all its dominions. He built dams and irrigated the land. He distributed clothes and food, and determined the amount of land and cattle to be given each man. An army of functionaries carried out his commands. Nobody could say, 'This is mine,' because everything belonged to the Sun. Labour was deemed sacred. The idle were put to death. In the spring the Son of the Sun went to the fields with his bulls and ploughed the first groove and planted the first grain of maize.

"The temples were stocked with grain, fabrics and spices. The Atlantian ships with their purple sails blazing the image of a snake holding the Sun in its teeth, sailed the seas and rivers of the world. Lasting peace was established on Earth. Men were forgetting the use of the sword.

"Then a cloud swept over Atlantis from the east.

"A yellow-faced, slant-eyed powerful tribe of Uchkurs dwelled upon the eastern plateaus of Asia. It obeyed a woman who was possessed. She was called Su Khutam Lu, which meant 'She who Speaketh to the Moon.'

"Su Khutam Lu told the Uchkurs:

" 'I shall take you to a land where the sun sets in a gorge between the hills. The sheep that graze there are as numerous as the stars; rivers of mare's milk flow there, and the tents are so big that a herd of camels can find shelter in them. Your steeds have not trodden their soil and you have not dipped your helmets in their rivers.'

"The Uchkurs swarmed down from the plateaus and fell upon the numerous nomad yellow-faced tribes. They subjugated them and became their war chiefs. They said to them, 'Follow us to the Land of the Sun of which Su Khutam Lu has spoken.'

"The nomads who worshipped the stars were fearless dreamers. They broke camp and drove their herds westward. Their march was slow, dragging on for years. In their van rode the Uchkur horsemen who attacked, fought, and destroyed the cities in their way. Their herds, and the carts of women and children, moved in their wake. The nomads by-passed India and poured into the eastern part of the European plain.

"Many settled on the banks of its lakes. The strongest, however, proceeded westward. On the Mediterranean coast they ravaged the first colony of Atlantians, and learned from their prisoners the lay of the Land of the Sun. In the meantime Su Khutam Lu died. They nailed her scalp to a tall pole and moved with this banner down the coast to the end of Europe where, from a mountain top, they beheld the Promised Land. A hundred years had elapsed since the Uchkurs left their native plateaus.

"The nomads felled trees in the forests and made rafts to cross the warm salt river. They set foot on the Promised Land of Atlantis, and fell upon the holy city of Tuleh. But when they climbed its high walls, they heard bells ringing in the city, and the chimes were so sweet that the yellow-skins would not destroy the city, nor touch its inhabitants, nor plunder its temples. They just replenished their stores and took clothes, and proceeded south-west. The dust raised by their carts and herds shut out the sun.

"Finally, the nomads were blocked by an army of red-skins. The delicate Atlantians were clad in gold and feathers of many shades, and were beautiful to behold. But they were no match for the nomad horsemen, who slew a great many and scattered the rest. When the yellow-skinned nomads tasted the blood of the Atlantians they were no longer merciful.

"Messengers were dispatched from the City of a Hundred Golden Gates to the redskins in the west, the Negroes in the south, the Aam tribes in the east, and to the cyclops in the north. Human sacrifices were made. Flames burned night and day on the temple tops. The city dwellers flocked thither to witness the sacrifices, to take part in the frenzied dances and orgies. They drank wine and squandered their treasures.

"The priests prepared themselves for the trials to come. They took the books of Great Knowledge to the mountain caves and buried them there.

"The outcome of the war was a foregone conclusion. The sated Atlantians put up a half-hearted defence of their wealth. The nomads, on the other hand, were fired with primeval greed and faith in their preordained success. Still, the struggle was prolonged and bloody. The country was laid waste. Hunger and the plague stalked the land. The armies overran and pillaged the country. The City of a

Hundred Golden Gates was taken by storm and its walls were torn down. The Son of the Sun leapt to his death from the top of the pyramid. The fires burning on the temple tops were extinguished. The surviving handful of learned men fled to the mountain caves. It was the downfall of civilization.

"Sheep now grazed in grass-grown squares between the ruined palaces of the great city, and yellow-faced shepherds sang sadly about the Promised Land, where the earth was blue and the sky was golden, so like the mirages they had seen in the steppes.

"The nomads asked their chiefs, 'Where shall we go now?' and the chiefs told them, 'We have brought you to the Promised Land. Settle here, and live in peace.' But many of the nomad tribes would not stay, and marched on westward, to the land of the Feathered Snake. There they were defeated by the sovereign Ptitligua. Other tribes made their way to the equator, and were wiped out by the Negroes, the herds of elephants, and the marsh fevers.

"The yellow-faced Uchkur chieftains elected the wisest among them to be the ruler of the conquered land. His name was Tubal. He had the walls repaired, the gardens cleared, the fields ploughed and the houses rebuilt. And he issued many wise and simple laws. He summoned the priests and sages who had fled to the caves, and told them, 'My eyes and ears are open to wisdom.' He appointed them as his advisers, permitted them to re-open their temples, and dispatched messengers to announce his desire for peace.

"Such was the beginning of the third and highest phase of Atlantian civilization. The blood of the numerous Atlantian tribes—black, red, olive and white—mingled with that of the dreamy hot-headed Asian nomads, the star-worshipping descendants of the possessed Su Khutam Lu.

"The nomads were soon assimilated by the other tribes. Nothing remained of their tents, herds and savage customs but songs and legends. A new tribe appeared, strong of build, with black hair and dark-yellow skin. The Uchkurs, descendants of the horsemen and war chiefs, were the aristocracy. They were fond of science, art and luxury. They put up a new wall with heptagonal towers round their city, coated the twenty-one ledges of their gigantic pyramid with gold, built aqueducts, and were the first in the history of architecture to erect columns.

"In protracted wars they re-conquered countries and cities that had split away. In the north they fought the cyclops—the wild descendants of the Zemze tribes who had not mixed with other races. Rama, the great conqueror, went all the way to India. He united the junior Arian tribes into the Kingdom of Ra. Thus, the boundaries of Atlantis were unprecedentedly extended and fortified, stretching from the lands of the Feathered Snake to the Asiatic coast of the Pacific Ocean, where the yellow-faced giants had once hurled stones at the Atlantian ships.

"The restless questing spirit of the conquerors yearned for knowledge. They read the ancient books of the Zemzes and the wise books of the Sons of Aam. One cycle closed, and a new one opened. Decayed remains of the 'Seven Papyruses of the Sleeper' were found in the caves. This discovery led to the rapid development of knowledge. The Sons of Aam had lacked creative zest. The Zemzes had lacked the ability of clear and keen reasoning. The restless and passionate Uchkurs possessed both these qualities in plenty.

"The fundamentals cf the new knowledge were as follows:

"'Man possesses the mightiest of forces, the matter of pure reason. But it is dormant within him. Just as an arrow released from a bow by a skilled hand strikes its target, so can the matter of dormant reason be released from the bow of will by the hand of knowledge. The power of directed knowledge is unlimited.'

"The science of knowledge was divided into two parts: the preliminary, which comprised the development of the body, will and mind, and the basic, which embraced knowledge of nature, the world, and the formulas by means of which the matter of directed knowledge harnessed nature.

"This consummation of knowledge and progress of a culture never again equalled on Earth continued for a century, from the 450th to the 350th year before the Flood, that is, before the end of Atlantis.

"Peace reigned on Earth. The powers of the Earth, called to life by knowledge, served man generously. The gardens and fields yielded bumper harvests. The herds multiplied. Labour was light. The people recalled their old customs and holidays, and there was nothing to hinder them from living, loving, giving birth and enjoying life. The chronicals called this era the *Golden* Age.

"A sphinx depicting the four elements in a single body—symbol of the mystery of dormant reason—was erected on the eastern boundaries of the Earth. Then man built the seven wonders of the world—a labyrinth, a colossus in the Mediterranean Sea, the pillars west of the Gibraltar, the stargazers' tower in Poseidon, the sitting statue of Tubal, and the city of the Lemutes on a Pacific Ocean island.

"The light of knowledge reached the black tribes that had been pushed back into the tropical marshes. The Negroes, civilized, built giant cities in Central Africa.

"The seed of Zemze wisdom produced wonderful fruit. But now the wisest of the wise realized that the original sin lay in the roots of civilization. Any further development of knowledge would lead to destruction. Mankind would slay itself even as the snake stings its own tail.

"The original sin lay in perceiving existence—the life of the Earth and its creatures—as something conceived by man's reason. In studying the world, man studied only himself. Reason was his only reality. The world was of his own conception, merely a dream of his. This concept of existence was bound to lead in each man's mind to the notion that he was the only being in existence, and the rest of the world nothing but the figment of his imagination. It was logical that a struggle for the single personality, a struggle of all against all, the extermination of mankind as of a dream that had turned against the man who dreamt it, would follow. Contempt and a loathing of existence as of a bad dream, a nightmare, were a natural sequel.

"This was the original fault of Zemze wisdom.

"Knowledge split in two. Some saw no way of extracting the seed of evil and said that evil was the sole power engendering existence. They called themselves the Black, since their knowledge stemmed from the black-skinned.

"Others, who thought evil was outside Nature, was but the deflection of reason from the natural, searched for a counteragent to combat it.

"They said, The Sun's ray falls on the Earth, perishes and is reborn in the fruits of the Earth. That is the fundamental law of life.' They likened reason to the ray. Its movement was descent, death in sacrifice and resurrection in flesh. The original sin, the solitude of reason, could, they said, be destroyed by the sin of the flesh. Reason must fall through flesh and pass the living gates of death. These gates were sex. Reason is destroyed by sexual craving, or Eros.

"Those who propounded this theory called themselves the White, for they wore linen tiaras, symbols of Eros. They instituted a spring holiday and played the mystery of sin in the luxuriant garden of the ancient Temple of the Sun. A virgin youth represented reason, a woman—the gate to carnal matter; and a snake represented Eros. People flocked from distant lands to see the play.

"The gap between the two schools of knowledge was great. A struggle ensued. An astounding discovery was made at the time. Man learned to release the vital force dormant in the seeds of plants. This fulminating, flame-cold material force, when released, soared up into space. The Black employed it as a weapon of destruction. They built huge flying-boats which struck terror into the hearts of their enemies. Savage tribes came to worship these flying dragons.

"The White realized that the end of the world was near, and prepared for it. They selected the purest and strongest from among the simple people and led them north and east. They gave them highland pastures, where they could live as primitives.

"The forebodings of the White came true. The Golden Age was on the decline; satiety came to the cities of Atlantis. Unbridled fancy, perversion, and depravity went unrestrained. The powers which man had mastered turned against him. Men became grim, vindictive and ruthless in face of inevitable perdition.

"Then came the last days. They were marked by a great calamity: the central region of the City of a Hundred Golden Gates was shaken by an earthquake. A large area of land sank below the surface of the ocean, and the waves of the Atlantic cut off the country of the Feathered Snake for all time.

"The Black blamed the White for having released the spirits of earth and fire with their invocations. The people were infuriated. Incited by the Black, they slaughtered more than half the populace wearing the linen tiara. Those who survived fled from the land of the Atlantians.

"The wealthiest citizens of the Black Order, called Magatsitls or the Ruthless, seized power in the City of a Hundred Golden Gates. They said:

" 'We shall destroy mankind because it is a nightmare of reason.'

"To enjoy the spectacle of death to the full, they announced festivals and games, opened the state treasury funds and shops to all, brought white maidens from the north and handed them over to the mob, threw open the doors of temples to all who thirsted for perverse pleasures, filled the fountains with wine, and roasted meat in the squares. A madness gripped the people. It was the time of the grape harvest.

"At night the Magatsitls came to the squares where the frenzied populace was gorging itself on food and drink, women and dances in the light of bonfires. They wore tall helmets with pointed combs and armoured belts, but carried no shields. With their right hands they hurled bronze bombs which burst into cold, destructive flames, and with their left they plunged their swords into the drunk and crazed.

"The bloody orgy was interrupted by a terrible earthquake. The statue of Tubal fell, the walls cracked, the pillars supporting the aqueduct tumbled over, and flames broke forth from deep cracks in the ground, shrouding the sky with ashes.

"Next morning the lurid disc of the sun shed its lustreless light over the ruins, the smouldering gardens, the crowds of maddened, life-weary, overgorged people, and piles of corpses. The Magatsitls climbed into their egg-shaped flying-ships and soared away through star-spangled space to the land of abstract reason.

"Many thousands of ships had left thus when a fourth shattering subterranean jolt shook the earth. A huge wave rose out of the ashen darkness in the north and rolled over the earth, swallowing up all living things in its path.

"Then a storm broke out and bolts of lightning struck the dwellings and the grounds around them. The rain came down in torrents, and volcanic rocks hurtled through the air.

"Sheltered by the walls of the great city, swarms of Magatsitls were still taking off from the top of the gold-layered pyramid. They swept through sheets of rain, smoke and ashes up into the starry skies. Three consecutive earthquakes rent the land of Atlantic asunder, and the City of a Hundred Golden Gates sank into the turbulent waves."

GUSEV OBSERVES THE CITY

Ikha was badly smitten. She obeyed Gusev's slightest command and gazed at him with love-dimmed eyes. It was both amusing and pathetic. Gusev was strict with her, but always just. When Ikhoshka languished under the stress of her pent-up emotions, he took her on his knee and stroked her head, scratched her behind the ear, and told her funny stories. She listened in a trance.

Gusev had made up his mind to escape to the city. The house was like a mousetrap to him. There was no chance to defend himself if the need arose, nor to get away. Yet Gusev was certain that Los and he were in grave danger. Los would not listen to him. He just frowned. The world was eclipsed for him by the skirt of the Tuscoob girl.

"No need to be so restless," he said. "What if they kill us? We're not afraid of death, are we? We could have stayed in Petrograd—much safer there."

Gusev had Ikhoshka bring him the keys to the hangar housing the flying-boats. He went there with a torch after dark, and spent the night tinkering with a little double-winged speed-boat. Its engine was simple enough The tiny motor worked on grains of white metal which disintegrated with incredible force under the effects of an electric spark. The machine received its electric charge from the air. Mars, Aelita had told them, was covered with high-tension electricity supplied by stations at both the poles.

Gusev dragged the boat to the hangar doors and returned the keys to Ikha. In case of need, he could wrench the padlock off.

Next he decided to take control of the city of Soatsera. Ikha showed him how to work the misty screen. It could be switched on one-way, so that he could see and hear without being seen or heard.

Gusev explored the entire city—its squares, the shopping district, the factories, and the workers' blocks. A strange kind of life passed before him on the misty screen.

The brick factory shops were low, dimly illumined by the light from the dusty windows. The wizened faces of the workers were despondent and sunken-eyed. Always, always the moving lathes, machines, bent figures, precise movements—it was a dismal, hopeless, ant-like existence.

Gusev saw the monotonous lines of workers' streets, and the same dismal figures trudging along them with drooping heads. Thousands of years of boredom wafted from those clean-swept brick passages, as alike as two drops of water. Clearly, hope had abandoned the people living in them.

Then the central squares appeared on the screen—buildings that rose like stepped pyramids, bright-green creepers, window-panes sparkling in the sun, well-dressed women, little tables and slim vases with flowers in the middle of the streets, eddying crowds of richly-attired people, men in black robes, the façades of houses—all reflected in the greenish parquet of the street. Golden flying-boats floated low over the city, casting fleeting shadows, and Gusev glimpsed upturned laughing faces and bright gossamer scarves.

The city led a double life. Gusev made a careful note of it. His experience told him that there must still be another, third, underground side to it. A great many carelessly-dressed young Martians loafed in the fashionable streets. They slouched about with their hands in their pockets and kept their eyes open. Gusev thought to himself, "Aha, I've seen the likes of you before."

Ikhoshka offered detailed explanations. But she refused point-blank to connect the screen with the building of the Supreme Council of Engineers.

She shook her red locks and clasped her hands in fear.

"Don't ask me to do it, Son of the Sky. Better kill me, precious Son of the Sky."

In the morning of their fourteenth day on Mars, Gusev took his seat in the armchair as usual, placed the switchboard on his knees, and pulled the cord.

A strange scene materialized on the screen. He saw clusters of alarmed, whispering Martians in the central square. The tables, flowers and bright parasols had all disappeared. A company of soldiers marched up in triangle formation like sinister stone-faced puppets. Then a crowd ran down a street of shops; a Martian spiralled up out of a scuffle in a winged machine. Similar groups of alarmed, whispering people clustered in the park. A crowd of workers at a factory stood scowling fiercely, their faces flushed with excitement.

Extraordinary things were afoot in the city. That was obvious. Gusev shook Ikhoshka by the shoulder: "What's going on?" She said nothing, her love-sick, dimmed eyes fixed on his face.

TUSCOOB

The city was in a state of unrest. The screen telephones hummed and flickered. Groups of Martians stood whispering in the streets, squares and parks. They were obviously waiting for something to happen, and kept looking up at the sky. There was a rumour that the storehouses of dry cactus were aflame. The water taps were opened in the city at noon, and the supply ran out—but not for long. There was an explosion south-west of the city. People pasted strips of paper crosswise on their windows.

The unrest spread from the centre of the city, the building of the Supreme Council of Engineers.

People spoke about the impending fall of Tuscoob's power, and the approaching changes.

"The lights will go off tonight."

The excitement was fanned by rumours.

word was repeated over and over. Los strained his ears. Like a muted bolt of lightning smiting his heart came the distant voice, repeating sorrowfully in an unearthly tone:

"Where are you, where are you, where are you, Son of the Sky?"

The voice died away. Los stared before him with dilated stricken eyes. Aelita's voice, the voice of love and eternity, the voice of yearning, reached him across the universe—calling, begging, imploring: "Where are you, where are you, my love?"

try and resolution to carry on had never been stronger.

The unrest subsided somewhat, but soon new rumours spread, one more terrifying than the other. One thing was known for certain. There was to be a head-on clash that evening in the Supreme Council between Tuscoob and Engineer Gor, the leader of Soatsera's workers.

After dusk, large crowds filled the vast square before the Supreme Council building. Soldiers guarded its stairs, entrances and roof. The cold wind had brought a fog, and the street lamps rocked in its moist clouds, diffusing a bleak red glimmer. The sombre walls of the building towered upwards into the darkness. All its windows were alight.

Seated under ponderous vaults on the benches of the amphitheatre in the round hall were the members of the Supreme Council. Their faces were alert and guarded. On a screen mounted high up on the wall they saw scenes snatched out of the teeming city—the interior of factories, street crossings with figures running to and fro in the fog, the contours of the reservoirs, the electro-magnetic towers, and the desolate rows of heavily-guarded storehouses. One by one, the screen contacted all the control mirrors in the city. The last to appear was the square outside the Supreme Council building—an ocean of heads shrouded in clouds of fog and the diffused light of the lanterns. The hall filled with the ominous rumbling noise of the crowd.

A shrill whistle called the council to order. The screen faded. Tuscoob stepped on the platform draped in black and gold brocade. He was pale, calm and resolute.

"There are disturbances in the city," he said. "They are aroused by the rumour that *I* shall be opposed today. This rumour was enough to shake the state. In my opinion this state of affairs is both cankerous and ominous. We must nip in the bud the reasons for all this excitement. I know that some of you will relay my words throughout the city tonight. I speak openly. The city is in the grip of anarchy. My agents say there are not enough muscles in the country to oppose it. We are approaching the end of the world."

The amphitheatre buzzed its protest. Tuscoob smiled scornfully.

"Anarchy, the force which is destroying the world order, stems from the city. Spiritual calm, the natural will to live, and man's powers of emotion are frittered away in the city on questionable entertainments and vain pleasures. The fumes of khavra are the soul of the city. Bright streets, noise, luxurious golden boats are the envy of those who see them from below. Women who bare their backs and bellies and wear tantalizing perfume; gaudy lights flashing across the fronts of brothels; boat-restaurants sailing above the streets—that's what the city is! Peace of mind goes up in smoke. The dissipated have just one wish—a thirst—a thirst for intoxication. But blood is the only thing that can intoxicate them."

Tuscoob jabbed the air before him with his finger. The men in the hall stirred again warily. He continued:

"The city is paving the way for the anarchist personality, whose sole aim and purpose in life will be destruction. People think anarchy is freedom. They are wrong. Anarchy thirsts for anarchy alone. It is the duty of the state to fight the disturbers of order—that is the law! We must oppose anarchy with our will for order. We must rally the sound elements of the country and send them out against anarchy with a minimum loss. We shall declare war on anarchy. The security measures taken so far are of a temporary nature, but the hour will come when the police reveals its most vulnerable spot. As we double the number of our police agents, the anarchists multiply fourfold. We must be the first to attack, and resort to a harsh but imperative measure: We must demolish the city."

Half the men in the amphitheatre howled and jumped to their feet. Their eyes burned. Their faces were pale. Tuscoob restored order with a single glance.

"The city will be destroyed—it is inevitable, one way or another. And it is best that we do it ourselves. I shall subsequently propose a plan of resettling the sound section of the city population in the countryside. We must use the rich land beyond the Liziazira Mountains, deserted since the civil war. Much will have to be done. But the cause is noble. We shall not manage to save civilization by destroying the city. We shall not even thereby postpone its end. But we *shall* help the Martian world to die with dignity and in peace."

"What does he say?" shouted the frightened men shrilly.

"Why must we die?"

"He's insane!"

"Down with Tuscoob!"

Tuscoob again restored order in the amphitheatre with a twitch of his brow.

"The history of Mars is drawing to a close. Life is waning on our planet. You know the birth and death rates. In a few more centuries the last of the Martians will watch the sun set for the last time. We are powerless to arrest the process of extinction. We must be wise and take firm action to grace the world's last days with luxury and joy. Our initial task is to destroy the city. It has done its duty to civilization. Now it is corrupting civilization and must perish."

Gor, the young broad-visaged young Martian Gusev had seen on the screen, rose from his place in the centre of the amphitheatre.

He had a low, rasping voice. His finger pointed at Tuscoob.

"He lies! He wants to destroy the city to keep his power. He condemns us to death to retain power. He knows that the only way he can retain power is to destroy millions of people. He knows how much he is hated by those who do not fly in golden boats, who live and die in the subterranean factory cities, who roam the dusty passages on holidays, yawning from despair, and who seek oblivion frenziedly in the accursed khavra. Tuscoob has made our deathbed. Let him lie on it himself. We do not wish to die. We were born to live. We know that Mars is doomed to extinction. But there is salvation—it will come from the Earth, the people of the Earth—a sound, fresh race with hot blood. He fears them. Tuscoob, you have hidden two men from the Earth in your home. You are afraid of them, the Sons of the Sky. You are strong only among the weak and khavra-doped. When strong hot-blooded men come, you will become a mere shadow—a nightmare. You will vanish like a phantom. That is what you fear most. Your theory of anarchy is a deliberate invention. You concocted your shocking plan for destroying the city on the spur of the moment. You thirst for blood yourself. You want to divert general attention so that you can do away with the two daring men who have come to save us. I know that you have issued an order to...."

Gor stopped short. His face turned purple from exertion. Tuscoob fixed him with his frowning eyes.

"I shan't stop—you can't make me!" Gor screamed. "I know—you practise ancient sorcery— But I'm not scared of your eyes."

With an effort he wiped the sweat from his

brow with his large palm. He took a deep breath, and staggered. The amphitheatre watched with bated breath as he dropped into his seat. His head fell on his arms. They heard him gnashing his teeth.

Tuscoob lifted his eyebrows and went on unperturbed:

"You say, depend on the immigrants from the Earth? Too late for that. Infuse new blood into our veins? Too late—too late and too cruel. We shall only prolong the agony of our planet. We shall only add to our suffering, for we shall inevitably become the slaves of our conquerors. Instead of meeting our end with dignity, we shall again enter the weary cycle of centuries. What for? Why should we, a frail and wise race, work for the conquerors? So that the life-hungry savages chase us out of our palaces and gardens, make us build new reservoirs, and dig for ore? So that the Martian plains resound again to battle-cries and our cities again breed perverts and madmen? No. We must die peacefully in our dwellings. Let Taltsetl shed its red rays from afar. We shall not admit foreigners. We shall build new stations at the poles and surround our planet with impenetrable armour. We shall destroy Soatsera—the nest of anarchy and delirious dreams. It was here, in Soatsera, that the criminal plan to contact the Earth was born. We shall run our ploughs across the squares. We shall leave nothing standing but the institutions we need to sustain life. And we shall make criminals, drunkards, madmen and day-dreamers work in them. We shall shackle them. They shall be offered the gift of life, for which they crave. Those who obey us shall get country holdings, means of livelihood, and comfort. Twenty millenniums of hard labour have given us the right to live in leisure, quiet and meditation. The end of civilization will be crowned by the Golden Age. We shall proclaim public holidays and organize wonderful entertainments. Perhaps we shall thus prolong our term for a few more centuries, since we shall live in peace."

The amphitheatre listened in silence, spellbound. Tuscoob's face had come out in spots. He closed his eyes as though to see into the future.

The low rumble of the thousands outside reached the vaulted hall. Gor rose. His face was contorted. He tore off his cap and hurled it aside. Holding his arms before him, he rushed down the aisle towards Tuscoob, seized him by the neck and pushed him off the brocaded platform. Then he turned his face to the amphitheatre, spread his hands out and shouted in a choking voice:

"Very well! If you want death, let it be death—but for you! We'll go on...."

The men on the benches jumped to their feet noisily. A few of them rushed to the prostrate Tuscoob.

Gor leapt to the door. He pushed aside the guard with his elbow. The hem of his black robe flashed in the door leading to the square. His voice resounded in the distance, echoed by the howling crowd.

LOS IS ALONE

"A revolution's started! The city's in an uproar! How d'you like that?"

Gusev was in the library. Merry sparks danced in his eyes. He had lost his sleepy look. His nose crinkled, and his moustache bristled belligerently. He thrust his hands deep under his leather belt.

"I've stowed away everything we need in the boat—food and hand-grenades. Even got one of their guns. Come on—chuck those books and let's go."

Los was huddled in the corner of his divan, looking at Gusev with unseeing eyes. He had waited for more than two hours for Aelita to appear, had been to her door and listened, but heard no sound. He had then returned to his seat and waited impatiently for the sound of her footsteps in the hall. He knew her light tread would thrill him to the core. She would enter, more beautiful and desirable than he imagined, and pass under the high sunlit windows, her black gown trailing over the mirror-like floor. And he would shiver. His whole soul would shudder and grow taut as before a storm.

"What's the matter with you? Feeling ill? I say let's go—everything is ready. I'll proclaim you Commissar of Mars. It's a clean job."

Los dropped his head to avoid Gusev's probing gaze. In a low voice he asked:

"What's happening in the city?"

"The devil knows. There's crowds of people in the streets. Hell of a noise. They're breaking windows."

"Go by yourself, Alexei Ivanovich. But come back tonight without fail. I promise you all my support. Make a revolution—make me Commissar. Shoot me, if you like, but leave me alone just now. Please."

"All right," said Gusev. "They're trouble-makers, they are, damn them. Fancy our coming all the way to seventh heaven to find a female waiting for us there. Bah! I'll be back at midnight. Ikhoshka will see to it that nobody gives me away."

Gusev left, and Los took up his book again.

"What's going to come of it?" he mused. "Will the storm sweep past? No, never. Did he welcome this feeling of waiting in agony for a super-light to smite him? No—there was no joy in his heart, nor sorrow; no dreams, no thirst, no satisfaction. But he felt life flowing into the cold loneliness of his body whenever Aelita was by his side. Life floated in, treading lightly on the mirror-like floor under the shining windows. But that too was no more than a dream. He wanted the consummation of his desire. Then life would flow into her too. Aelita would attain completion. And he—he would be left again to yearn in solitude."

Never had Los felt so strongly the futility of ardent love. Never had he understood so well love's delusion—that terrible sacrifice of self to woman—the bane of man. You flung open your arms, spread your hands from star to star, waiting for woman. And she came and took—and lived. As for you—lover and father—you were left suspended like an empty shell, your arms spread from star to star.

Aelita was right. He should not have learned so much—he knew too much. He, Son of the Earth, still had hot blood racing through his veins; he was still filled with the disturbing seeds of life. But his mind was a thousand years away, in another land. He knew what he need not have known. His mind was a yawning abyss. What had his reason discovered? An abyss, and new mysteries beyond it.

Make a singing bird basking in the glorious rays of the sun shut its eyes and try to fathom the merest particle of human wisdom, and it will drop dead.

The whistle of the departing flying-boat reached his ears. Ikha's head bobbed in through the library doorway.

"Son of the Sky, dinner is ready."

Los hastened to the dining-room—a white circular chamber where he was accustomed to dine with Aelita. It was hot there. The flowers in the tall vases under the columns exuded a warm aroma. Looking away so that Los would not see her tear-stained eyes, Ikha said:

"You dine alone, Son of the Sky."

She covered Aelita's plate with white flowers.

Los's eyes clouded. He sat down to table gloomily. He did not touch his food—just fingered his bread, and drank several glasses of wine. A faint sound of music issued from the mirror-inlaid cupola over the table. Los clenched his teeth.

Two voices—those of a string and a brass instrument—poured from the cupola, merging, interweaving and singing of dreams that would never come true. They parted on the highest, dying notes, and were back instantly in the low registers, calling yearningly from the tomb, beckoning, singing of reunion, blending, whirling—much like an old, old waltz.

Los gripped his slim wine-glass. Ikha hid behind a column, covering her face with the edge of her dress. Her shoulders were shaking. Los threw down his napkin and rose from the table. The haunting melody, the stuffy flowers, and the wine—all of it was so futile.

He asked Ikha:

"Can I see Aelita?"

Ikha shook her red locks, still hiding her face. Los gripped her shoulder.

"What's happened? Is she ill? I must see her."

Ikha slipped out of Los's grip and fled, dropping a photograph. Los picked it up. It was a picture of Gusev in full military dress—cloth helmet, shoulder belt, one hand on the hilt of his sabre and the other holding a revolver. Behind him were exploding grenades. The card was signed: "To little Ikhoshka with everlasting love."

Los dropped the photograph, walked out of the house and strode across the meadow to the copse. He was advancing in leaps quite unconsciously, and muttering:

"She needn't see me if she doesn't want to. To think I travelled to another world—an unparalleled effort—just to sit on a couch and wait for a woman to come out and smile at me. Preposterous! Mad! Gusev's right—I'm sick. Doped, waiting for a tender glance. To blazes with it."

His thoughts stabbed painfully. He groaned as though he had a toothache. Unwittingly, he leapt high in the air and barely kept his feet. His white hair streamed in the wind. He loathed himself thoroughly.

He ran towards the lake; it lay as smooth as a mirror. Sheaves of sunlight gleamed on its blue-black surface. It was hot. Los gripped his head and sat on a stone.

Purple globular fish rose indolently from the translucent depths of the lake, twitching their long needles and staring indifferently at Los with watery eyes.

"D'you hear me, little fish—pop-eyed, silly fish?" Los murmured. "I am calm—and I say it in full command of my senses. I am tormented by curiosity—I yearn to take her in my arms when she enters in her black robe. I want to hear her heart beat. She'll come close to me, so shyly. I'll see her eyes grow wild. You see, little fish—I've stopped. I'm not going on. I'm not thinking. I don't want to. That's enough. The thread is torn—it is the end. Tomorrow I shall go to the city. Fight? Splendid. Death? Excellent. But no music, please—no flowers, no temptations. I cannot stand the hothouse atmosphere. That magic ball in her hand—to blazes with it! It is all deceit, phantoms."

Los rose, picked up a large stone and hurled it into a shoal of fish. His head was splitting. The light hurt his eyes. Beyond the copse jutted the peak of a glittering snow-capped mountain. "What I need is some cold air." Los screwed up his eyes at the diamond peak and set out for it through the blue grove.

The trees receded and he came out on to a desolate hilly plateau. The ice-coated pinnacle was far beyond its edge. He strode on, kicking at heaps of slag and rubble. All around gaped mine shafts. Los resolved doggedly to bite into that snow glittering in the distance.

A cloud of brown dust rose in a distant dell. The sultry wind carried the sound of many voices. From a hilltop Los saw a large group of Martians trudging along a dry canal bed. They were carrying picks and hammers, and knives fastened to the ends of long sticks. They stumbled as they walked, shaking their weapons and bellowing fiercely. Circling high over the clouds of dust in their wake were large birds of prey.

Los remembered what Gusev had told him about the disturbances in the city. He thought, "Live, struggle, conquer, perish—but keep your heart on a leash, the mad unhappy thing."

The Martians disappeared behind the hills.

Los hurried on, agitated by his thoughts. Suddenly he stopped short and jerked his head back. A flying-boat was descending from the blue sky. It circled, glittering above him, lower and lower, then slid over his head and landed.

Someone wrapped in snow-white fur stood up in the boat. He recognized Aelita's worried eyes peering out from under the fur trimmings of her helmet. Los's heart pounded, sending currents of heat through his body. As he approached the boat, Aelita pushed the moist fur away from her face. Los fixed his yearning eyes on her.

"I have come for you. I was in the city. We must flee. I have been longing for you so much...."

Los gripped the side of the boat and heaved a sigh.

THE SPELL

Los sat behind Aelita. The pilot, a red-faced youth, sent the flying-boat up smoothly into the air.

The cold wind tore at them. Aelita's white fur coat smelled of mountain gales and snow.

She turned to look at Los, her cheeks glowing.

"I saw Father. He ordered me to poison you and your companion." Her teeth gleamed. She unclenched her fist. A tiny stone flask dangled from a ring on her finger. "Father said, 'Let them die in peace. They deserve a tranquil death.' "

Aelita's grey eyes filled with tears. But she laughed and pulled the ring off her finger. Los grasped her hand.

"Don't throw it away," he said, taking the flask from her and putting it in his pocket. "It is your gift, Aelita; a dark drop—sleep, peace. Now you are both life and death to me." He put his face close to hers. "When the terrible hour of solitude comes, I shall feel you again in this drop."

Aelita closed her eyes and rested her back against him in her effort to understand. But it was no good—she could not understand. The roaring wind, Los's hot chest against her back, his hand resting on her shoulder under the fur—it seemed their blood was coursing through a single artery. And they experienced a single sense of delight, flying as a single body towards some sparkling primeval recollection. But no, it was no good—she could not understand.

A minute or more passed. The boat was approaching the Tuscoob estate. The pilot glanced over his shoulder: Aelita and the Son of the Sky looked so strange. Tiny sun-sparks glittered in the pupils of their eyes. The wind ruffled the snowy fur of Aelita's coat. Her eyes gazed ecstatically at the ocean of sky all round.

The young pilot poked his sharp nose into his collar and chuckled noiselessly. Banking the boat on her left wing and diving, he set her down beside the house.

Aelita came out of her spell. Her fingers fumbled with the bird-head buttons of her coat as she tried to get it unfastened. Los lifted her out of the boat, set her down on the grass and stood leaning over her. Aelita said to the boy-pilot:

"Bring out the closed boat."

She did not see Ikhoshka's red eyes or the scared pumpkin-yellow face of the house steward. Smiling and turning to Los absent-mindedly on the way, she led him to her rooms at the back of the house.

It was his first visit to Aelita's quarters. The chambers were vaulted, had golden arches, and their walls were covered with shadow pictures like the silhouettes on a Chinese parasol. The warm spicy air went to his head.

Aelita said softly:

"Sit down."

Los obeyed. She sank to the floor at his feet, put her head on his knees and sat very still.

He looked down at the ashen hair combed high on her head, and placed his hand over hers. Her throat trembled. Los bent over her. She said:

"Are you bored with me? Forgive me. I do not know how to love yet. It is all so vague. I told Ikha, 'Put more flowers in the dining room when he is alone, and let the ulla play for him.' "

Aelita rested her elbows on his knees. She had a dreamy look.

"Did you hear me? Did you understand? Did you think of me?"

"You must surely know," he said, "that when I do not see you I go mad with alarm. And when I do see you I am even more alarmed. It seems to me that it was my yearning for you that drove me across the stars."

Aelita sighed. She looked happy.

"Father told me to poison you, but I could see that he did not trust me. He said, 'I shall kill both of you.' We have not long to live, but don't you feel the minutes opening endlessly, blissfully?"

She relapsed into silence as she saw Los's eyes gleam with cold resolution, his mouth set in an obstinate line.

"All right," he said, "I shall fight."

Aelita moved closer and whispered:

"You are the giant of my youthful dreams. You are handsome. You are strong. You are brave and kind. Your hands are iron. Your knees are stone. Your glance is deadly. It makes women feel heavy under the heart."

Aelita's head rested lightly on his shoulder. Her murmuring became indistinct, barely audible. Los brushed the hair from her face.

"What is it?"

Impetuously, she wound her hands round his neck, like a child. Large tears welled up in her eyes and streamed down her little pointed face.

"I do not know how to love," she said. "I have never known. Pity me. Do not shun me. I shall tell you stories. I shall tell you about the terrible comets, and the battle of the airships, and the end of the beautiful land beyond the mountains. You will never be bored. Nobody ever caressed me. When I saw you the first time, I thought, 'He is the giant of my childhood dreams.' I wanted you to lift me in your arms and take me away. It is gloomy here, hopeless. Like death itself. The sun gives little warmth. The snows on the pole do not thaw any longer. The seas are drying up. There is nothing but endless desertland. Tuma is covered with copper sands. The Earth, the Earth—dear giant, take me to the Earth. I want to see the green hills, the waterfalls, the clouds, the big animals and the giants. I do not want to die."

Aelita burst into tears. She was like a little girl—amusing and delightful when she clapped her hands as she spoke of the giants.

Los kissed her wet eyes. She grew quiet. She pouted her small mouth. She gazed up at the Son of the Sky with loving eyes, beholding her fairy giant.

Suddenly a low whistle pierced the semi-darkness of the room and the oval screen on Aelita's dressing table lit up softly. Tuscoob's head was peering at her.

"Are you there?" he asked.

Aelita jumped like a cat on to the carpet and ran to the screen.

"I am here, Father."
"Are the Sons of the Sky still alive?"
"No, Father. I gave them poison. They are dead."
Aelita spoke in a cold, sharp voice. She stood with her back to Los, hiding him from her father.
"What else do you want me to do, Father?"
Tuscoob did not reply. Aelita's shoulders heaved and her head rolled back. Her father snarled viciously:
"You lie! The Son of the Sky is in the city. He's leading the uprising!"
Aelita swayed. Her father's head disappeared.

THE SONG OF LONG AGO

Aelita, Ikhoshka and Los took off in a four-winged boat for the Liziazira Mountains.
The electro-magnetic wave receiver—the mast with the wires—operated unceasingly. Aelita, bent over a tiny screen, listened and watched.
She found it difficult to make anything out in the medley of frantic telephone messages, calls, shouts, and worried inquiries that

whirled in the magnetic fields of Mars. Still, Tuscoob's steely voice managed to cut through and dominate the chaos. The shapes of a disturbed world flitted across the mirror.

On several occasions Aelita heard a strange voice bellowing:

"Comrades, don't listen to the whisperers. We want no concessions. To arms, comrades, the hour has struck—all power to the Sov—Sov—Sov. . . ."

Aelita turned around to face Ikhoshka.

"Your friend is bold; he is a true Son of the Sky. Have no fears about him."

Ikhoshka stamped her feet like a goat and shook her red head. Aelita saw that their flight had remained undiscovered. She took the earphones off and wiped the misted pane of the porthole with the palm of her hand.

"Look," she said to Los, "the ikhi are following us."

The boat was flying high over Mars. Two animals with scabrous coats of brown hair and webbed wings flew in the glaring light on each side of the boat. Their flat horny beaks faced the portholes. Catching sight of Los, one of them dived and struck its beak against the pane. Los jerked his head back. Aelita laughed.

They soon left Azora behind. Below were the sharp cliffs of the Liziazira Mountains. The boat lost height, flew over Lake Soám and landed on a broad ledge hanging over an abyss.

Los and the pilot dragged the boat into a cave, hoisted the luggage baskets on to their backs and followed the women down a barely perceptible time-worn stairway leading to the gorge. Aelita tripped along lightly in front. Holding on to projections in the rocks, she looked at him intently. Stones flew from under his large feet, echoing hollowly in the gorge.

"This is where Magatsitl carried his staff with the skein of wool," said Aelita. "You'll now see the sacred ring of fire."

Midway down the precipice the steps turned into a narrow tunnel in the cliff. Its dark recesses had a dank smell. Scraping the rock with his shoulders and bending double, Los advanced laboriously between the polished walls. He groped for, and found Aelita's shoulder, and at once felt her breath on his lips. He whispered in Russian, "Sweetheart."

The tunnel issued into a dimly-lit cave. Basalt columns glittered all around. Thin clouds of vapour ascended at its far end. Water gurgled somewhere, and there was the monotonous sound of drops falling from the dark vaults.

Aelita led the way. Her black cape and pointed hood floated over a lake, and kept disappearing behind the clouds of vapour. Her voice reached Los from the darkness. "Careful," she called, and then appeared on the narrow steep arch of an ancient bridge. Los felt the arch shake under his feet, but saw nothing but the cape floating through the semi-darkness.

It grew lighter. The crystals overhead glimmered faintly. The cave ended in a colonnade of low stone pillars beyond which opened a view of the rocky pinnacles and mountain reservoirs of Liziazira bathed in the rays of the evening sun.

The columns faced a broad terrace overgrown with rusty moss. Its edge hung over an abyss. Almost invisible steps and pathways led up to a town of caves. In the centre of the terrace stood the Holy Threshold, half submerged in soil and overgrown with moss. It was a large sarcophagus built of blocks of gold. Crude images of birds and beasts ornamented it on all sides, and on top of it lay the Sleeping Martian—one hand under his head, the other pressing an ulla to his breast. The ruins of a colonnade encircled this curious sculpture.

Aelita sank to her knees before the Threshold and kissed the place over the Sleeping Martian's heart. When she rose to her feet, her face was pensive and gentle. Ikha also squatted at the feet of the Sleeping Martian, embracing and pressing here face to them.

On their left there was a golden triangular door wedged in between a rocky wall covered with half-obliterated inscriptions. Los pulled out the clumps of moss covering it and opened the door with difficulty. Inside was the ancient abode of the custodian of the Threshold —a dark cave with stone benches, a hearth and a couch carved of granite. They put their baskets in the cave. Ikha covered the floor with a mat, made Aelita's bed, poured some oil into a lamp hanging under the ceiling, and lit it. The young pilot went off to guard his winged boat.

Aelita and Los sat on the edge of the abyss. The sun was setting behind the craggy summits. Long black shadows stretched along the hills, broken by yawning clefts. It was a dismal place, barren and wild, these mountains where the ancient Aols once sought refuge from men.

"Long ago the mountains were covered with vegetation," said Aelita. "Herds of khashi used to graze here and waterfalls rumbled in the gorges. Tuma is dying. The cycle of the millenniums is closing. Perhaps we are the last Martians—when we're gone, Tuma will be lifeless."

Aelita fell silent. The sun disappeared behind the neighbouring dragon-backed cliffs. Its glowing crimson poured into the heavens, merging with the purple dusk.

"But my heart tells me otherwise." Aelita rose and walked along the edge of the precipice, picking up dry moss and sticks. Having gathered a pile in her cape, she returned to Los and built a fire. Then she fetched a lamp from the cave, got down on her knees, and lit the moss with its flame. Soon the fire was crackling merrily.

Now Aelita sat down, took a little ulla from under her cape, and propping her elbows on her raised knees, began to pluck at its strings. The instrument emitted a gentle droning sound. Aelita lifted her head to the stars twinkling in the nocturnal sky and sang in a low, sad voice:

Gather the dry grass, the dung of beasts and the broken branches.
Pile them up neatly,
Strike stone against stone—woman, leader of two souls.
Strike a spark, and the fire will burn.
Sit at the fire, hold thy hands to the warmth.
Thy husband sits across the dancing flames.
Through the smoke rising to the stars
The eyes of thy man gaze into the darkness of thy being, the depths of thy soul.
His eyes are brighter than the stars, hotter than the fire, bolder than the luminous eyes of Cha.
Know thee—the sun will be a cold ember, the stars will
Roll off the Sky, and wicked Taltsetl will no longer burn over the world—
But thee, woman, will sit at the fire of immortality, thy hands close to its flames,
And listen to the voice of those yet to come to life,
The voice in the darkness of thy womb.

The fire was dying. Dropping the ulla on her knees, Aelita gazed at the coals—they illumined her face with their warm glow.

"It is our ancient custom," she said sternly, "for a woman who sings the song of the ulla to a man, to become his wife."

LOS FLIES TO GUSEV'S AID

At midnight Los climbed out of the flying-boat into the courtyard of the Tuscoob estate. The windows in the house were dark. Gusev had obviously not returned yet. The slanting wall was bathed in starlight. The bluish reflections of the constellations glittered in the black windowpanes. Behind the merlons of the roof loomed an angular shadow. Los peered at it—what could it be?

The young pilot leaned over anxiously and whispered:

"Don't go there."

Los pulled his Mauser out of its holster. His nostrils quivered as he inhaled the chilly air. His memory pictured the fire at the edge of the abyss, the smell of burning moss, and Aelita's glowing eyes. "Will you come back?"

she had asked, standing by the fire. "Do your duty—fight, conquer. But do not forget—it is all no more than a dream—shadows. Here, by the fire, you live, and will not die. Be sure to come back." She had moved close. Her eyes next to his seemed to open into the bottomless night filled with stardust. "Come back—come back to me, Son of the Sky."

The memory singed him, and flickered out—it had lasted no more than a second while he had unbuttoned the holster. Peering at the strange shadow looming over the roof on the other side of the house, Los felt his muscles tighten, his hot blood pounding—fight, fight!

He ran lightly towards the house, stopped to listen for a moment, then crept along the side wall and peeped round the corner. A smashed airship was lying on its side near the entrance to the house. One of its wings projected over the roof. Los made out several sack-like objects on the grass. They were corpses. The house was dark and mute.

Was Gusev among them? Los examined the corpses.

No, they were Martians. One of them sprawled face down on the steps. Another lay among the debris of the ship. They had evidently been shot down by guns fired from the house.

Los ran up the steps. The door was slightly ajar. He went inside.

"Alexei Ivanovich!" he called.

There was no answer. He switched on the lights. The whole house came ablaze. Then he thought, "That's asking for trouble," but dismissed the thought the next moment. Under one of the arches he slipped over a sticky pool.

"Alexei Ivanovich!" he called again.

No answer. He entered the narrow room with the misty screen, sat down in an armchair and dug his finger-nails into his chin. Should he wait for Gusev there? Or fly to his aid? But where to fly? Whose ship had been shot down outside? The dead did not look like soldiers. They were more like workers. What had the fighting been about? Had Gusev been there? Or Tuscoob's men? Yes, he must hurry.

He picked up the switchboard and plugged in the "Square of the Supreme Council Building." He pulled the cord, and was thrown back by the roar that invaded the room. There were clouds of smoke, tongues of flame and sparks in the reddish gleam of the lanterns.

Somebody's body suddenly shot up with flapping arms and a blood-smeared face.

Los pulled the cord and turned away from the screen.

"He should at least let me know where to look for him in this mess."

Los clasped his hands behind his back and paced the low-ceilinged room. Suddenly he halted, swung round, and whipped out his Mauser. A head was showing in the door just above the floor—a red-haired, copper-skinned, wizened head.

Los leaped to the door. A Martian lay in a pool of blood in the passage. Los picked him up and put him in a chair. His stomach was ripped open.

Licking his lips, the Martian muttered:

"Hurry, we are perishing, Son of the Sky, save us. Open my hand...."

Los pulled a note out of the dying Martian's fist. It was scarcely legible.

"Sending a ship and seven workers for you. Reliable chaps. Am storming the Supreme Council building. Land your ship on the square by the tower. Gusev."

Los bent over the wounded Martian. He asked him what had happened, but the Martian only wheezed and jerked.

Los took his head in his hands. The wretch stopped wheezing. His eyes bulged. An expression of horror in them gave place to one of bliss. "Help...." His eyes glazed over, and his mouth set in a grin.

Los buttoned his coat and wrapped his scarf round his neck. He went to the front door and opened it. Jets of blue flame hissed from behind the carcass of the wrecked ship. A bullet sent Los's helmet flying.

Gnashing his teeth, Los dashed towards the ship, and putting the weight of his body behind the heave, upset it on the men hiding behind it.

The mangled heap of metal crashed to the ground, and the Martians behind it squealed in terror. The huge wing swayed dangerously, then fell on top of the men crawling from under the debris. Bent figures scurried in zigzags across the misty green. Los took a leap forward and fired. The report was deafening. The nearest Martian dived into the grass. Another flung away his gun, squatted and covered his face with his hands.

Los gripped him by the collar of his silver coat and lifted him like a puppy. He was a soldier. Los said:

"Did Tuscoob send you?"

"Yes, Son of the Sky."
"I shall kill you."
"Do as you wish, Son of the Sky."
"Where is your ship?"
Dangling in front of Son of the Sky's terrible face, the Martian motioned with dilated eyes in the direction of the trees; a small fighter stood in their shade.
"Did you see the Son of the Sky in town? Can you find him?"
"Yes."
"Off we go."
Los jumped into the ship. The Martian took his seat behind the controls. The propeller whirred and the nocturnal wind lashed at their faces. The huge wild stars swayed in their black heights.

GUSEV'S ACTIVITIES

Having taken off from Tuscoob's estate at about 10 a.m. equipped with an air map, a gun, some provisions and six hand-grenades, which he had brought with him from Petrograd unknown to Los, Gusev sighted Soatsera at noon. The central streets were empty. Military ships and troops were placed in three concentric semi-circles in the enormous star-shaped square fronting the Council of Engineers building.

As Gusev began his descent, he was noticed, and a shiny six-winged ship took off from the square and zoomed into the air, flashing gaily in the sunshine. Silvery figures were ranged on its decks. Gusev described a circle over the ship and pulled a grenade carefully out of his sack.

Below him, the ship's coloured wheels were revolving and its mast-wires bristling.

Gusev bent over the side of his boat and shook his fist at the ship. There was a faint answering wail. The little silver figures aimed their short guns at him, and out of little yellow puffs came bullets ripping at the side of Gusev's boat. Gusev cursed lustily. He pulled a lever and swooped down on the ship. As he sped over them he threw his grenade. There was a deafening explosion. Straightening out his boat, he turned round to look. The ship, somersaulting giddily, was falling to pieces in mid-air. It crashed on to the roofs below.

That was when things began to happen.

Flying over the city, Gusev recognized the squares, the government buildings, the arsenal and the workers' quarters he had seen on the screen. Thousands of Martians seethed like a disturbed ant-hill in the vicinity of a factory wall. As Gusev landed, the crowd scattered in all directions. He touched ground on a cleared spot, and grinned.

The Martians recognized him. Thousands of hands were raised in greeting. The crowd chanted, "Magatsitl! Magatsitl!" They edged closer to him warily. He saw their trembling faces, their pleading eyes, their radish-red bald heads. These were the workers, the rabble, the poverty-stricken.

Gusev climbed out of his boat, swung his sack on his shoulder and waved his hand.

"Greetings, comrades!" The stillness that ensued seemed unreal. Gusev towered like a giant among the frail shapes of the Martians. "What did you come here for, comrades? To talk, or to fight? If it's talking you're after, I'm off. So long."

A sigh rose from the crowd. A few Martians yelled in despair and the rest chimed in:

"Help—help us, Son of the Sky!"

"You're going to fight, then?" Gusev asked, and added in a hoarse voice: "The fight's on.

A warship attacked me just now. I blew it to bits. To arms, men, follow me!"

Gor (Gusev recognized him at once) elbowed his way through the crowd. He was grey with agitation. His lips were trembling. He clawed at Gusev's chest.

"What are you talking about? Where do you want us to go? They will wipe us out. We have no arms. We must resort to other measures. . . ."

Gusev tore Gor's hands from his chest.

"The chief measure's to act. The one who acts will seize power. I haven't come here all the way from the Earth to talk to you. I came to teach you to act. You're moss-grown, Comrades Martians. Those who aren't afraid to die—follow me! Where's your arsenal? To arms! Follow me to the arsenal!"

"Ai-yai!" shrieked the Martians.

The Martians pressed forward, jostling and crushing each other. Gor spread his hands in despair.

The uprising had begun. A leader had been found. Heads were whirling. The impossible seemed possible. Gor, who had been preparing the uprising slowly and methodically, but who had hesitated before making a decision even after the events of the day before, now suddenly came to life. He made twelve burning speeches, transmitted to the workers' quarters over the misty screens. Forty thousand Martians flocked to the arsenal. Gusev divided the rebels into small groups and stationed them under cover of the buildings, monuments and trees. He arranged for the women and children to be placed before all the control screens registering the events in town for the government's benefit, and told them to curse Tuscoob in a half-hearted manner. This Asiatic ruse fooled the government for a while.

Gusev feared an attack from the air. To divert attention and gain time, he sent five thousand unarmed Martians to the centre of the city to yell for warm clothes, bread and khavra. He told them:

"None of you will return alive. Remember that. And now, off you go."

Five thousand Martians wailed, "Ai-yai!" opened enormous umbrellas inscribed with slogans, and marched off to die, whining an old, forbidden song:

Under the glazed roofs,
Beneath the iron arches,
In a jug of stone

Rise the fumes of khavra.
We are very merry, oh!
Hand us the jug of stone!
Ai-yai! We shall not return
To the mines and quarries,
We shall not return
To the ghastly tomb-like passages,
To the machines, the machines.
We want to live! Ai-yai! To live!
Hand us the jug of stone!

Whirling their enormous umbrellas and wailing, they disappeared in the narrow streets.

The arsenal, a low square building in the old section of the city, was guarded by a small military detachment. The soldiers stood in a semi-circle on the square in front of a bronze gate. Behind them were two curious machines made of wire spirals, discs and spheres (Gusev had seen one like them in the deserted building). The rebels approached and surrounded the arsenal by way of crooked little by-streets. It sheer walls were strong.

Running from tree to tree and peering round corners, Gusev studied the location and found that the best way to attack the arsenal was from the gate in front. He had his men wrench one of the bronze entrance doors out and bind it with ropes. Then he told the rebels to swarm down to the building and scream "ai-yai" at the top of their voices.

The soldiers guarding the gate had been calmly watching the crowds milling in the by-streets, but now they pushed their machines a little forward. A purple light flickered from the spirals. Pointing to them, the Martians screwed up their eyes and piped, "Beware of them, Son of the Sky!"

There was no time to lose.

Planting his feet apart, Gusev gripped the ropes and lifted the bronze door. It was heavy, but he could carry it. He made his way under cover of the wall to the edge of the square. The gate was just a few dozen steps away. Whispering the command, "Make ready," he mopped his face with his sleeve, thinking, "If I could only get real angry," and held the door before him like a shield.

"Come on, laddies!" he yelled hoarsely, panting as he advanced across the square.

Several bullets struck his makeshift shield. Gusev staggered. Now he grew angry in earnest and increased his pace, cursing as he went. All around the Martians screamed and wailed as they came pouring from behind the corners, gateways and trees. A deafening explosion rent the air. But the avalanche of Martians passed on, crushing the soldiers and the dreaded machines.

Cursing vehemently, Gusev dashed up to the gate and rammed at the lock with the corner of his bronze door. The gate gave way. Gusev rushed into the square courtyard where four-winged ships were standing in rows.

The arsenal was captured. Forty thousand Martians received arms. Gusev contacted the Council of Engineers building by the screen telephone and demanded the surrender of Tuscoob.

The government dispatched a flight of airships to attack the arsenal. Gusev flew out to meet it with his fleet. The government airships turned back. Gusev and his fleet gave chase and shot them down over the ruins of ancient Soatsera. The ships crashed at the feet of the gigantic statue of Magatsitl smiling with closed eyes. The rays of the setting sun gleamed on his scaly helmet.

The sky was now controlled by the insurrectionists. The government centred its police force round the Council building. Machines which ejected round lightning were installed on its roof, and soon part of the insurrectionists' fleet was shot down by them. Towards nightfall, Gusev stormed the square of the Supreme Council and put up barricades in the streets radiating starwise from the square. "I'll teach you to make a revolution, you brick-red devils," he muttered, showing the Martians how to wrench stone blocks out of the pavements, fell trees, tear doors off their hinges and fill their shirts with sand.

They turned the two arsenal lightning machines round to face the Supreme Council building and pelted the government troops with flaming shells. The government charged the square with electricity by means of an electric magnet.

Then Gusev made his last speech of the day—very brief and expressive—from the top of a barricade, and hurled three hand-grenades in succession. The force of their explosion was terrifying: three shafts of flame shot up. The square was enveloped in clouds of dust and acrid smoke. Howling, the Martians rushed forward. (This was the scene Los had glimpsed on the screen in Tuscoob's house.)

The government removed the magnetic field, and now fiery round shells soared over the square, bursting into flashes of bluish flame. The dark pyramidal houses were shaken by the thunderous detonations.

The battle did not last long. Gusev dashed across the corpse-strewn square at the head of a picked detachment and burst into the Supreme Council building. It was empty. Tuscoob and the engineers had escaped.

EVENTS TAKE A NEW TURN

The mutineers seized all the important points in the city indicated by Gor. It was a cool night and the Martians froze at their posts. Gusev ordered bonfires to be lit. This was unheard of—no fires had been burned in the city for a thousand years, and the Martians knew of the dancing flames only from the songs of old.

Gusev lit the first fire, using broken furniture for firewood, in front of the Supreme Council building. "Ulla, ulla," the Martians whimpered, clustering round the fire. One after the other bonfires blazed up in all the squares. Their ruddy glow cast flickering shadows on the inclined walls of the buildings, and glimmered in the window-panes.

Bluish faces appeared at the windows. They peered out in alarm and agony at the strange fires and the dismal ragged figures of the rebels. Many houses were deserted that night.

It was quiet in the city. There was no other sound but the crackling of the fires and the clanking of weapons, as though the millenniums had retraced their march and had begun their wearisome advance all over again. Even the shaggy stars over the streets and fires were different—the men sitting round the fires involuntarily raised their heads to gaze at their forgotten pattern. Gusev surveyed his troops from his winged saddle. He dropped from the starry heights on to the square and cast a great shadow as he crossed it. He was a true Son of the Sky, a titan stepped down from a stone socle. "Magatsitl, Magatsitl," the Martians whispered in superstitious awe. Many were seeing him for the first time, and crawled up to touch him. Others sobbed like children, saying, "Now we won't die. We shall be happy. Son of the Sky has brought us life."

The emaciated bodies covered with dusty overalls, the wizened, sharp-nosed, haggard faces, the sad eyes trained for centuries to see nothing but whirling wheels and dark mine shafts; the skinny hands, unskilled in movements of joy and daring—the hands, faces and eyes reflecting the sparks of the fires—they were all reaching out to the Son of the Sky.

"Splendid, chaps. Keep your chins up," he told them. "There's no law to make you suffer till doomsday. Never you fear. When we win out, things will be fine."

Late that night, Gusev returned to the Council building. He was cold and hungry. Some two-score heavily-armed Martians were sleeping on the floor under the low golden arches of the vaulted hall. The mirror-smooth surface of the floor was spattered with chewed khavra. Gor was sitting on a stack of cartridge tins in the centre of the hall, writing in the light of his searchlight. The table was littered with open tins, flasks and breadcrumbs.

Gusev perched on a corner of the table and began to devour the food ravenously. Then he wiped his hands on his trousers, drank from a flask, grunted, and said in a hoarse voice:

"Where's the enemy? That's what I want to know...."

Gor raised his inflamed eyes and glanced at the blood-stained rag tied around Gusev's head, at his broad, strong-champing jaws, his bristling moustache, his distended nostrils.

"Nobody tells me where the hell the government troops have gone," Gusev continued. "There's about three hundred of 'em scattered out there in the square, but they had about fifteen thousand soldiers all told. Vanished. They're not needles, you know, to vanish in a haystack. If they'd have disappeared, I'd know about it. We're in a tight hole. Any moment the enemy can turn up behind our back."

"Tuscoob, the government, the remnants of the troops and part of the population have gone down into the labyrinth of Queen Magr beneath the city," said Gor.

Gusev jumped to his feet.

"Why in blazes didn't you say so at once?"

"It's useless to attempt to follow Tuscoob. Sit down and eat, Son of the Sky." He frowned as he produced a pepper-red packet of dry khavra from his robe, put some in his mouth and chewed slowly. His eyes grew misty and dark, and the wrinkles smoothened on his face. "Several thousands of years ago we did not build big houses, because we could not heat them—we had not as yet discovered electricity. In winter, the people descended deep under the ground. The huge halls we built in the natural caverns—the columns, tunnels and passages—were all warmed by the subterranean heat of the planet. The heat in the craters was so intense that we used it to produce steam. We still have a few primitive steam engines of those days on some of our islands. The tunnels joining the subterranean cities stretch throughout the planet. It is no use looking for Tuscoob in that labyrinth. He is the only one who knows the plan and secret passages of the labyrinth of Queen Magr, the ruler of two worlds who reigned over the whole of Mars. The network of tunnels under Soatsera leads to 500 populated cities and more than a thousand dead ones. There are stores of arms and airship hangars everywhere. Our forces are scattered and we are poorly armed. Tuscoob has an army and he is backed by the landowners, khavra planters and all those who, after the devastating war of thirty years ago, became proprietors of city houses. Tuscoob is clever and treacherous. He provoked these events in order to stamp out all vestiges of resistance. The Golden Age—the Golden Age!"

Gor shook his dazed head. Purple spots spread over his cheeks. The khavra was beginning to take effect.

"Tuscoob dreams of the Golden Age. He wishes to open the last era of Mars—the Golden Age. Only the elect, only those deserving of bliss would have access to it. Equality is unattainable; there is no such thing as equality. Universal happiness is the pipedream of khavra-doped madmen. Tuscoob said, 'The thirst for equality and universal justice destroys the greatest achievements of civilization.'" A pink foam appeared on Gor's lips. "Back to inequality, to injustice! Let the past centuries swarm down upon us like flies. Shackle the slaves, chain them to the machines, the lathes, drive them down the mineshafts—to wallow in grief. And the blessed will wallow in joy. The Golden Age! Grit and gloom. Damn my father and mother. Why was I ever born, may I be damned!"

Gusev looked at him, chewing his cigarette savagely.

"Bah. You've certainly made a mess of things!"

Gor said nothing for a long time. He sat huddled over the cartridge tins like a very old man.

"You're right, Son of the Sky. We of ancient Tuma have not solved the riddle. Today I saw you fighting. You're full of fire! You are vigorous and reckless. It is for you, Sons of the Earth, to solve the riddle. But not for us. We are too old. We are filled with ashes. We have let time slip through our fingers."

Gusev tightened his belt.

"All right, say it's ashes. What do you propose to do tomorrow?"

"Tomorrow morning we must locate Tuscoob over the screen telephone and approach him on the question of mutual concessions."

"Look here, comrade, you've been talking nonsense for a whole hour," Gusev cut in. "Here's the layout for tomorrow: you'll announce to Mars that power is in the hands of the workers. Demand unconditional subordination. I'll pick out a few good lads and go straight to the poles with my fleet. I'll capture the electromagnetic stations and wire at once to the Earth—to Moscow—for reinforcements. They'll have apparatuses ready in six months, and it'll take them only. . . ."

Gusev lurched and gripped the table for support. The whole building was shaking. Pieces of carved ornaments dropped from the dark shadows of the ceiling. The Martians on the floor leapt to their feet and looked around in bewilderment. Another jolt shook the building. It was stronger than the first. The window-panes crashed on to the floor and the doors flew open. A low rumble rolled through the hall. From the square came the sounds of shooting and screaming.

The Martians clustering in the doorways suddenly fell back. The Son of the Sky—Los —strode into the hall. He was almost unrecognizable. His large eyes were dark and sunken, and they emitted a strange light. The Martians backed away and squatted on their haunches. His white hair was standing on end.

"The city's surrounded," he said in a loud firm voice. "The sky is teeming with ships. Tuscoob is blowing up the workers' districts."

THE COUNTER-ATTACK

Los and Gor had just rushed out on to the front steps under the columns of the building when a second explosion rent the air. A blue fan of flame burst in the northern section of the city, followed by clouds of smoke and ashes. Before the thunderous reverberations had died away a storm swept down upon them. A dark-red glow seeped over the sky.

Not a single shout came from the star-shaped square filled with troops. The Martians watched the fire in silence. Their houses and families were burning to ashes. Their last hopes went up in black smoke.

After a short conference with Los and Gor, Gusev made arrangements to get his air fleet in readiness. All the ships were in the arsenal. There were only five giant dragon-flies on the square. Gusev sent them up on a reconnaissance flight. The ships mounted into the sky, their wings glowing red in the light of the conflagration.

He received word from the arsenal that the troops were embarking on their ships. Meanwhile, the fires were spreading. It was ominously still in the city. Gusev sent his messengers to the screen telephone to hasten the embarkation, and ran back and forth across the square like a huge shadow, yelling hoarsely and forming the scattered troops into columns. Returning to the steps, he scowled and twitched his moustache.

"Will you tell those"—a strange expression followed which Gor could not understand—"at the arsenal to hurry up."

Gor returned to the telephone. Finally a telephone message came through that the embarkation had been completed and the ships were taking off. A few moments later the dragon-flies glided low over the city through the thick smoke. Standing with his feet planted apart and his head thrown back, Gusev viewed the V formations of the ships with pleasure. And then the city was shaken by a third explosion.

Tongues of blue flame licked through the lines of the ships. The dragon-flies shot up, spun and vanished, leaving nothing but a rain of ashes and clouds of smoke.

Gor came out on to the steps. His head had sunk into his shoulders and his face was twitching. When the noise died down, he said:

"The arsenal's blown up. The fleet's wiped out."

Gusev grunted and chewed his moustache. Los leaned against a column and stared at the conflagration. Gor stood up on his toes to peer into Los's glassy eyes.

"This is going to end badly for those who remain alive."

Los said nothing. Gusev shook his head obstinately and stalked down to the square. He gave a command, and soon column after column marched away along the streets towards the barricades.

In another moment Gusev's winged shadow was flying over the square and shouting from above, "Hustle, you half-baked devils, get a move on with you!"

The square was soon empty. The conflagration which had spread over a large section of the city now illumined formations of dragon-flies flying over the city from the opposite direction. These were Tuscoob's ships.

Gor said:

"Run, Son of the Sky, you can still save yourself."

Los shrugged his shoulders. The ships were approaching and losing height. One fiery ball after another shot up out of the dark of the streets to intercept them. These were the round balls of lightning fired by the mutineers' machines. The lines of winged galleys described a circle over the square and split up to sail in different directions over the streets and roofs. The incessant bursts of fire illumined their sides. One galley turned over, dropped and caught its wings between the roofs of two buildings. Others landed on the square and spewed forth soldiers in silver jackets. The soldiers ran down the streets. They were fired at from the windows and from behind corners, and pelted with stones. More and more ships kept coming over, casting an unending line of fiery shadows on the square.

Los saw Gusev's broad-shouldered figure climbing up on to the terrace of a house. Five or six ships immediately swerved towards him. He lifted a large stone over his head and hurled it at the nearest galley. Then the flashing wings covered him on all sides.

Los was shaken out of his torpor. He dashed across the square to the house. The ships circled above, spitting fire and roaring. Los gritted his teeth, noting everything round him with a sharp eye.

He cleared the square in a few leaps and espied Gusev up on the terrace, crawling all over with Martians, heaving like a bear under their scrambling legs and arms, shaking them off and hammering at them with his fists. He wrenched one off his throat and threw him into the air, dragging the others with him as he moved along the terrace. Then he fell down.

Los cried out in alarm. Clinging to the ledges of the building he climbed on to the terrace. Gusev's bleeding mouth and bulging eyes appeared again from under the squealing writhing mass. Several soldiers sprang upon Los. He shook them off with loathing, and then began to pick the soldiers off Gusev and hurl them like so many sticks over the railing. The terrace soon emptied. Gusev tried to rise, but only rolled his head from side to side. Los picked him up, jumped into the open door and put him down on the carpet of the little room illumined by the red glow outside.

Gusev was breathing hoarsely. Los looked out of the door. The ships were gliding past the terrace—he saw the sharp-nosed faces peering out of them. He was certain they would attack again.

"Mstislav Sergeyevich," Gusev called. He was sitting up, feeling his head and spitting blood. "Our men have been wiped out—the whole lot of 'em.... Can you imagine it—swarming down on us and killing us like flies.... If anybody's alive, he's in hiding. Left me all alone. Oh, damn it!" He got to his feet, staggered across the room and stood before a bronze statue of some eminent Martian. "You just wait!" He picked it up and made for the door.

"What on earth are you doing?"

"I can't stand it, see? Let me go!"

He ran out on to the terrace. Spurts of fire jetted from under the wing of a ship floating past. Then there was a thud and a crash.

"Aha!" shouted Gusev.

Los dragged him back into the room and slammed the door shut.

"Alexei Ivanovich, can't you understand—we're beaten—it's all over. We must save Aelita."

"All you think about is your damned wench."

Gusev sat down abruptly, clutched his head, snorted and stamped his foot.

"All right," he snarled, bursting with impotent fury, "let them skin me! Nothing's right in the world. Nothing's right on this planet! 'Save us,' they said, 'please save us....' Hung on for dear life, they did.... 'We want to live,' they said. To live! But what could I do? I shed my blood, but they crushed us all the same. Damn it, I can't stand the sight of it. I'll tear those despots of theirs to pieces."

He snorted again and stamped to the door. Los gripped his shoulders, shook him and fixed him with a stern eye.

"This is a nightmare. Come. We may be able to get back. Home—back to Earth."

Gusev smeared the blood and dirt over his face.

"Let's go."

The room opened on to a circular landing hanging over a deep shaft. A spiral staircase wound to the bottom. The dim light of the conflagration outside filtered through the skylight down into the dizzy depths of the shaft.

Los started down the narrow stairs. It was quiet below. But above them the firing had grown louder and they heard the bottoms of the ships scraping against the roof of the building. It looked as though the Martians were attacking this last refuge of the Sons of the Sky.

Los and Gusev ran down the endless spiral stairs. It grew darker. Suddenly they saw a small figure below. It was crawling towards them laboriously. Then it stopped and cried weakly:

"They'll break in at any moment. Hurry. The entrance to the labyrinth is at the bottom."

It was Gor, wounded in the head. Licking his lips, he said:

"Keep to the big tunnels. Watch the signs on the walls. Good-bye. If you return to Earth, tell them about us. Perhaps you will be happy on Earth. But for us, there is nothing but ice deserts, death and agony. Aye, we've let our chance slip by. We should have loved life furiously and ardently—ardently...."

There was a noise above. Gusev rushed down the stairs. Los wanted to take Gor along, but the Martian clenched his teeth and gripped the bannister.

"Go. I want to die."

Los hurried down after Gusev. At last they reached the circular landing from which the steps led steeply to the bottom of the shaft. Here they found a large flagstone with a ring screwed into it. They lifted it with difficulty: a stream of dry air wafted up from the dark gap.

Gusev slipped into it first. As he replaced the block of stone over his head, Los saw figures of soldiers appearing far above in the reddish dusk of the circular landing. They came running down the steps. Gor stretched his hands out to them and fell under their blows.

QUEEN MAGR'S LABYRINTH

Los and Gusev groped their way through the musty darkness.

"There's a turn here, Mstislav Sergeyevich."

"Is it a narrow tunnel?"

"No, it's wide."

"Here are some more columns. Hold on, there! Where are we?"

They had been in the labyrinth for no less than three hours. Their matches had run out. Gusev had dropped his searchlight in the fighting. They crept along in utter darkness.

The tunnels branched out endlessly, crossing and receding away into the depths. There was the clear and monotonous sound of dripping water. Their dilated eyes discerned some vague greyish outlines in the distance, but these hazy spots were only a hallucination.

"Stop!"

"What's the matter?"

"There's no bottom here."

They stood still and listened. A fragrant, dry breeze fanned their faces. There was the sound of breathing coming from somewhere very far, very deep below. They sensed, with vague alarm, that there was nothing before them Gusev groped for a pebble and threw it into the darkness. A few seconds later they heard the faint thud of the pebble as it struck the bottom.

"It's a well."

"But what's breathing down there?"

"Can't tell."

They turned and came up against a wall. Both to the right and left their hands fumbled at crumbling cracks and arches. The edge of the invisible well was very close to the wall —to the right, to the left, and again to the right. They soon realized they were turning round and round and could not find the tunnel by which they had come to the narrow cornice.

They stood close to each other, shoulder to shoulder, their backs against the rough surface of the wall, listening to the hypnotizing sighs issuing from the depths of the well.

"Is this the end, Alexei Ivanovich?"

"Looks like it."

After a moment's silence Los asked in a strange voice, very softly:

"Look—do you see anything?"

"No."

"To the left, in the distance."

"No, no."

Los whispered something to himself and shifted from one foot to the other.

"Love life furiously and ardently—that's the way...."

"What are you talking about?"

"About them. And about us."

Now Gusev shifted his feet and sighed.

"There it is, breathing. Do you hear it?"

"What—death?"

"Who the devil knows what it is? I've thought a lot about it," Gusev went on, as though discoursing with himself. "When you're lying prone in a field with your gun, and it's dark and raining—no matter what you think about it always comes down to one thing—death. You picture yourself lying at the wayside like a dead horse, frozen, and grinning in death. I don't know what'll happen after I die—I just don't know. But I've got to know while I'm still alive: am I a man or a piece of rotting horseflesh? Or is it all the same? When the time comes to die and I roll my eyes up, shudder and give up the ghost, will the whole world—at that moment—everything I've seen with my eyes, turn upside down, eh? Will the thing lying dead and grinning be me—me, so alive and remembering all the way back to when I was three years old—

while the whole world goes rolling on just the same as before? That's what I'm afraid of. I can't understand it. We got so used to killing ever since nineteen fourteen that a man meant nothing to us—you put a bullet through him—and there he was. No, it's not as simple as all that. Once I lay wounded on a cart, looking up at the stars. I felt sick at heart. What's the difference, I wondered, whether I was a louse or a man? A louse has to eat and drink the same as me. It's just as hard for a louse to die as for me. The end's the same for both of us. But then I saw the stars twinkling like diamonds up there in the sky—it was the month of August. And my innards shuddered. I felt as though all those stars were inside of me. No, I wasn't a louse. No. And I cried like a baby. Why was the world made like that? A man isn't a louse. It's a terrible thing to do, a great sin, to crack a man's skull. And people have invented poison gases too. I want to live, Mstislav Sergeyevich, I can't stand this damned darkness. What are we waiting for anyway?..."

"It is here," said Los in the same strange voice.

At that moment the endless tunnels reverberated with the sound of a crash in the distance. The cornice underfoot and the wall behind them shook. Stones came falling through the darkness. The rumble rolled on in waves and died in the distance. It was the seventh explosion. Tuscoob had kept his word. Judging from the remoteness of the detonation, they had left Soatsera far behind.

Stones kept tumbling around them for some time. Then it grew quiet. Gusev was the first to notice that the breathing in the depths had ceased. Now new strange noises were issuing from the bottom of the well—a kind of hissing and bubbling, as though a soft liquid were coming to a boil. Gusev could stand it no longer—spreading his arms along the wall, he moved away, shouting, cursing and kicking at the stones.

"The cornice goes around. Do you hear? There must be an exit here. Ooph, bumped my head against something!" For a while he groped in silence, then his agitated voice came from somewhere ahead of Los who was still standing motionless against the wall: "Mstislav Sergeyevich—there's a handle here. It's a knife-switch—hurrah!—a knife-switch!"

There was a screeching sound, and a dusty

light went on under the low brick cupola. The ribs of its flat vault were supported by the narrow ledge of the cornice hanging over a circular shaft some 10 metres in diameter.

Gusev was still clutching the handle of the knife-switch. Los hugged the wall on the other side of the shaft, under the arch of the cupola. He shielded his eyes from the glare with his hand, then removed it and peered down into the shaft. He bent low to see to its bottom. Gusev saw his hand shake, as though he were trying to throw something off his fingers. When he raised his head, his hair was standing on end and his eyes were dilated with horror.

Gusev shouted:

"What is it?" He looked down into the depths of the brick-walled shaft. There was a dark brown skin writhing at the bottom. It was making that hissing noise, a bubbling that was growing ever more ominous. The skin swelled and bulged. It was dotted all over with large horse eyes focussed on the light, and shaggy paws....

"It's death!" screamed Los.

It was a crawling mass of spiders. They had probably been breeding in the warm recesses of the shaft, and the explosion had disturbed them and caused them to swarm up the shaft. They were making that hissing, rustling sound. One of the spiders came crawling out on to the cornice.

Los was standing near by. Gusev shouted:

"Run!" He jumped over the shaft, grazing his head against the vault of the cupola, landed on his haunches near Los, grabbed his hand and pulled him towards the tunnel entrance. They ran as fast as their legs would carry them.

There were dusty lamps burning under the ceiling of the tunnel at rare intervals. A thick layer of dust covered the floor. There were remnants of columns and statues, and narrow doorways leading to other tunnels. Gusev and Los reached the end of the passage which brought them out to a hall with a flat vault and low columns. In its centre stood a broken statue of a woman with a fleshy, fiercely scowling face. Beyond were a number of dark niches. Dust lay everywhere, on the statue of Queen Magr and the shattered fragments of domestic utensils.

Los stood still with glassy, dilated eyes.

"There are millions of them there," he said, looking over his shoulder. "They are waiting—biding their time until the day comes for them to overrun and govern life on Mars. . . ."

Gusev drew him away into the largest tunnel leading from the hall. Here the lamps also burned dimly at rare intervals. They moved along it for a long time, passing an arched bridge over a broad well, at the bottom of which lay the carcasses of gigantic machines. The dusty grey walls led on and on. They were gripped with despair, ready to drop with fatigue. Los kept repeating in a low voice:

"Let me go, I want to lie down."

His heart was pounding. He stumbled after Gusev in the dust, racked with anguish. Drops of cold sweat streamed down his face. Los had seen the yawning fangs of Death, and yet a greater force was making him hold on to life, and he staggered on through the endless empty passages.

Suddenly the tunnel swerved sharply and Gusev gasped. The indigo-blue, dazzling sky and the glittering ice-capped mountain peak which Los remembered so well opened before them, framed in the arch of the tunnel. They emerged from the labyrinth in the vicinity of Tuscoob's estate.

KHAO

"Son of the Sky," called a high-pitched voice.

As Gusev and Los approached the estate from the side of the copse, a little sharp-nosed face popped out from behind the blue foliage. It was Aelita's pilot, the little lad in the grey coat. He clapped his hands and danced, wrinkling his face until it looked like a tapir's. Pushing aside the branches, he pointed to a winged boat hidden among the ruins of the reservoir.

He told them that the night had passed quietly, that he had heard a distant explosion at daybreak, and had seen the smoke of a big fire. Thinking the Sons of the Sky had perished, he had climbed back into his boat and flown to Aelita's retreat. She had also heard the explosion and watched the fire from the height of her cliff. She told him to go back to the estate and wait for the Son of the Sky. "If Tuscoob's servants seize you," she had said, "die in silence; if the Son of the Sky is dead, find his corpse, search his clothes for a little stone flask, and bring it to me."

Los listened to the youth's tale with clenched teeth. Then he went with Gusev to the lake to wash off the bloodstains and dust. Gusev carved a club almost the size of a horse's leg out of a branch of hard wood, after which they all got into the boat and climbed into the luminous blue.

Gusev and the pilot dragged the boat into the cave, lay down near its entrance and unfolded a map. At that moment Ikha came tripping down from the cliff above. She clapped her hands as she glimpsed Gusev, and tears welled up in her loving eyes. Gusev laughed happily.

Los hurried down the precipice leading to the Holy Threshold. He felt as if the wind were blowing him down the steep steps, through the narrow passages and across the little bridges. What was in store for Aelita and him? Would they escape with their lives or not? He could not think—his thoughts died before they had time to take shape. What was most important now was that he would again behold her, "born of the light of the stars." His only wish was to gaze at the thin little blue face and forget himself in a flood-tide of joy.

As he ran through the clouds of steam rising over the bridge spanning the lake in the cavern, Los glimpsed again the moonlit view of the mountains beyond the low columns. Cautiously he made his way to the broad ledge overhanging the abyss. The golden Holy Threshold glimmered dully. The air was hot and still. A wave of tenderness suffused his whole being—he wanted to kiss the copper moss, the footprints on this last retreat of love.

Deep below jutted the barren edges of the hills. The ice shone against the dark blue of the sky. His heart was gripped with yearning. Here were the ashes of the fire, the crushed grass where Aelita had sung the Song of the Ulla. A crested lizard scuttled by, hissing over the stones. It stopped and turned its head to look at him.

Los opened the triangular door in the rock and entered, stooping low.

Aelita was asleep among her white pillows in the light of the lamp hanging from the ceiling. She lay on her back, her bent arm above her head. Her thin little face was sad and sweet, and her closed eyelids trembled, disturbed by a dream.

Los went down on his knees at the head of her couch and gazed rapturously at the mate of his joy and sorrow. What torments would he not go through now to keep sadness away from this dear face, to save this young sweetness from destruction. As she breathed, a lock of ashen hair on her cheek rose and fell gently.

Los thought of the blood-curdling sight of those breathing, rustling, hissing creatures in the deep well of the labyrinth, biding their time. A groan of anguish burst from his lips. Aelita sighed and woke up. She stared blankly at Los for a moment, then her eyebrows lifted in amazement. Supporting herself with both hands, she sat up.

"Son of the Sky," she said tenderly and softly. "My son, my love."

She did not hide her nakedness; only a blush of girlish self-consciousness tinged her cheeks. Her bluish shoulders, budding breasts, and narrow hips seemed born of the light of the stars. Los remained on his knees before her, looking mutely at his love, filled with an overwhelming joy. Her bitter-sweet perfume wrapped him in a tempestuous haze.

"I dreamt of you," said Aelita. "You were carrying me in your arms up some glass steps, higher and higher. I heard your heart beating as the blood surged in and out. I was filled with languor. I waited for you to stop, for my yearning to cease. I want to learn to love. I know only the stress and anguish of languor. You have aroused me." Her eyebrows lifted still higher. "You look so strange. Oh, my giant!"

She moved back to the far corner of her couch. Her lips opened like those of a little animal at bay. Los said hoarsely:

"Come to me."

She shook her head.

"You look like the terrible Cha."

He covered his face with his hand, trembling from the fierce effort to restrain himself. The next moment he was all aflame. He took his hand away, and Aelita asked softly:

"What is it?"

"Don't be afraid."

She moved closer to him and whispered again:

"I am afraid of Khao. I shall die."

"Don't be afraid. Khao is fire—it is life. Don't be afraid of Khao. Come to me, my love!"

He reached his arms out to her. Aelita sighed inaudibly. Her eyelashes fell and her strained little face became drawn. Then she suddenly rose and blew out the lamp.

Her fingers buried themselves in Los's snowy hair.

There was a noise outside the cave, as of a swarm of bees droning. Neither Los nor Aelita heard it. The droning grew louder. Then a warship rose like a giant wasp from the abyss and grazed the rock with its prow.

The ship hung in the air level with the ledge. A step-ladder fell over its side. Tuscoob and a company of soldiers clad in armour and corrugated helmets disembarked.

The soldiers stationed themselves in a semicircle in front of the cave. Tuscoob went up to the triangular door and struck it with the end of his staff.

Los and Aelita were fast asleep. Tuscoob turned round and pointed to the cave with his staff.

"Take them," he snapped.

ESCAPE

The warship circled over the cliffs of the Holy Threshold for some time, then flew off towards Azora, and landed somewhere. Only now were Ikha and Gusev able to rush down to the Threshold. They found Los lying prone in a pool of blood near the cave entrance.

Gusev lifted him—Los was not breathing. His eyes were shut and his chest and head were caked with blood. Aelita was gone. Ikha wailed as she gathered up her mistress's things. She found everything but the hooded cape—the kidnappers had apparently wrapped Aelita, dead or living, in it and borne her away to the ship.

Ikha made a bundle of what remained of the one who was "born of the light of the stars." Gusev heaved Los over his shoulder and they retraced their steps across the bridges over the bubbling dark waters, down the steps of the precipice wrapped in mist—the path trodden by Magatsitl carrying a spinning-wheel and the striped apron of an Aol maiden, the sign of peace and life.

Gusev dragged the boat out of the cave above, and put Los in it. He tightened his belt, pulled his helmet down over his eyes and said sternly:

"They won't catch me alive. And if I ever get back to Earth—we'll return. . . ." (Three incomprehensible words followed.) He climbed into the boat and gripped the controls. "You go home, you two. And remember me kindly." He leaned over the side and shook hands with the pilot and Ikha. "I'm not asking you to come with me, Ikhoshka; don't know whether I'll come out of this alive. Thanks, dear girl, for your love. We Sons of the Earth never forget such things. Believe me. Good-bye."

He screwed his eyes up at the sun, nodded, and took off. Ikha and the lad in the grey fur coat stood watching the Son of the Sky flying away. They did not notice the winged dot mounting from beyond the lunar cliffs in the west to intercept him. When Gusev disappeared in the rays of the sun, Ikha flung herself on the mossy rocks in such despair that the lad was frightened—had she too departed from sad Tuma?

"Ikha, Ikha," he sobbed, "kho tuah mirra-tuah murra...."

Gusev did not see the warship flying to intercept him. He checked his map and fixed his eyes on the cliffs of the Liziazira floating past, holding his course due east, where the spaceship lay hidden in the cactus grove.

Behind him reclined Los's body, wrapped in a sheet which flapped in the wind. It was motionless as if he were asleep. At least it did not have the frightening limpness of a corpse. Gusev suddenly realized how much he cared for his comrade.

What had happened was this: Gusev, Ikh-oshka and the pilot had been sitting in the cave near the boat, enjoying a bit of fun, when suddenly they heard the sounds of shots below. Then a scream. Next moment a warship veered up like a hawk from the abyss, leaving Los's lifeless body behind on the ledge. It circled above the cliff, watching.

Gusev spat overboard—he was fed up to the gills with Mars. If he could only get to the spaceship and pour some vodka down Los's throat. He touched Los's body—it was still warm. "Maybe he'll come round yet." Gusev knew from experience the impotence of Martian bullets against the human body. "But he ought to have come out of his faint by now." Alarmed, he looked over his shoulder at the sun. That was when he saw the ship swooping down on him from above.

Gusev veered north to avoid it. The ship turned in the same direction. Yellow puffs darted from it. Gusev began to climb, intending to double his speed when losing height, and make his getaway.

The icy wind whined in his ears and tears filmed his eyes and froze on his eyelashes. A flock of loathsome ikhi, flapping their wings haphazardly, made for the boat, but missed it and fell behind. Gusev had lost his orientation long ago. The blood pounded in his temples and the rarefied air whipped him with icy thongs. Gusev dived. The warship fell far behind, and was soon swallowed up by the horizon.

There was nothing but copper-red desertland below as far as the eye could see. Not a single tree, nor any signs of life anywhere, nothing but the shadow of the boat sliding over the flat hills, the sandy waves, the cracks in the glittering stony soil. The ruins of houses cast their gloomy shadows here and there on the hills. And everywhere the land was cleft by the ribbons of dry canals.

The sun was setting behind the smooth edge of the sandy plain; its copper rays shone dismally, and still there was nothing in sight but the waves of sand, the hills, and the crumbling ruins of dying Tuma.

Night fell swiftly. Gusev descended and landed on a sandy plain. He climbed out of the boat, uncovered Los's face, raised his eyelids, pressed his ear to his heart. Los was neither dead nor alive. Gusev noticed an open flask dangling on the chain from a ring on Los's little finger.

"Damn this desert," said Gusev, walking away from the boat. The icy stars blinked in the limitless black skies. The sand was grey in their light. It was so quiet that he heard the sand running into the depressions made by his footsteps. His throat was parched and he felt terribly homesick. "Damn this desert!" He went back to the boat and took his seat behind the controls. What course should he take? The pattern of the stars was so strange and unfamiliar.

Gusev switched on the motor, but after a few revolutions, the propeller whirred to a stop. The explosive powder fuel had run out.

"Oh, all right," Gusev muttered. He got out of the boat, thrust his club under his belt and pulled Los out of the cockpit. "Let's go, man," he said, hoisting Los on to his back. He set out, sinking ankle-deep in the sand. At long last he came to a hill. He put Los down on the steps of a staircase. Glancing up at the hill, he saw a solitary column bathed in starlight looming high on the hill-top. He flung himself on the ground. His blood throbbed with an overpowering weariness.

He lost all sense of time. The sand chilled him, froze his blood. Finally he sat up and lifted his head in anguish. Low over the desert hung a grim reddish star. It was like the eye of a large bird. Gusev stared at it open-mouthed.

"The Earth." He lifted Los and ran towards the star. He now knew where the spaceship lay.

Breathing hard and sweating profusely, Gusev jumped across the ditches, yelling wildly as he stumbled over the stones, and kept on running doggedly. The dark horizon so close ahead receded as he ran towards it. Now and then he would lie down and press his face to the cool sand to moisten his parched lips with its vapours. Then he would pick up his comrade again and plod on, glancing from time to time at the reddish rays of the Earth. His huge shadow moved in solitude over the cemetery of the world.

The crescent Olla pushed its edge over the horizon. Then, at midnight, the round Likhta floated up, shedding a mild silvery light. The sand dunes now cast a double shadow. The two strange moons sailed over the sky—one upwards, the other down. Taltsetl faded in their light. The ice-bound summits of Liziazira loomed in the distance.

At last Gusev came to the end of the desert. It was almost daybreak. He entered the cactus grove. Kicking down a plant, he greedily devoured its jelly-like watery meat. The stars faded. Rose-edged clouds appeared in the violet sky. He suddenly became aware of a monotonous hammering of metal against metal resounding clearly in the morning stillness.

Gusev soon realized its meaning. He caught sight of three netted masts—they belonged to the warship which had pursued him. That was where the sounds were coming from. The Martians were destroying the spaceship.

Gusev broke into a run under cover of the cactuses. He saw the warship alongside the large rusty hump of the spaceship. Two dozen Martians were pounding at its studded coat with big hammers. It looked as though they had just begun. Gusev put Los on the ground and pulled out his club.

"Hey, you so-and-so!" he yelled. He rushed up to the warship and smashed its metal wing with a single blow of his club, struck off its mast and hammered against the hull like mad. Soldiers came jumping out of its interior. Throwing away their weapons, they dropped overboard like peas and scattered in all directions. Whining and squealing, the soldiers crawled away into the thickets. The grove was deserted in a flash—so great was their terror of the invulnerable omnipresent Son of the Sky.

Gusev unscrewed the lid over the porthole, dragged Los in, and the two Sons of the Sky disappeared into the egg. The lid slammed shut. Then the Martians hiding behind the cactuses witnessed a singularly remarkable sight.

The huge rusty egg broke into a roar, and billows of brown dust and smoke spurted from under it. Tuma quaked from the thunderous detonations. Roaring and screeching, the gigantic egg leapt over the cactus grove, hung for a moment in a cloud of dust, then shot into the sky like a meteor, bearing the fierce Magatsitls back to their native land.

OBLIVION

"Well, Mstislav Sergeyevich, are we still alive?"

Something scalded Los's mouth. He felt a liquid fire pouring through his body—his veins and bones. He opened his eyes. A little dusty star was twinkling above—just within reach. The sky had a strange look about it. It was yellow and padded. Something was beating rhythmically, and the dusty star trembled above.

"What time is it?"

"Worse luck—the watch's stopped," a voice replied.

"Have we been flying long?"

"We have, Mstislav Sergeyevich."

"Where are we flying?"

"The devil knows. I can't make out a thing. There's nothing but the darkness and the stars. We're rocketing through space."

Los closed his eyes, trying to probe the emptiness of his memory, but found nothing there and fell back into an impenetrable coma.

Gusev tucked the blankets round him and turned back to the observation tubes. Mars was already smaller than a saucer. Its dry sea bottoms and the dead deserts formed lunar spots on its surface. The disc of sand-swept Tuma diminished; the spaceship was flying farther and farther away from it into the pitch-black void. Now and then the ray of a star pricked Gusev's eye. But try as he did, he could see no red star anywhere.

Gusev yawned and snapped his jaws—he was tired of all this cosmic void. He checked the supplies of water, food and oxygen, wrapped himself in a blanket, and lay down on the vibrating floor next to Los.

When he woke up from a pressing feeling of hunger, he had no idea how much time had elapsed. Los was lying next to him with open eyes—his face haggard, sallow and old. He asked quietly:

"Where are we?"

"Same place as before—space."

"Alexei Ivanovich, have we been on Mars?"

"Seems your mind's gone blank."

"Yes, something's the matter with me. Just when things start coming back to me, my memory breaks off in the strangest way. I don't know what's happened—it's all like a dream. Give me a drink."

Los shut his eyes and asked tremulously: "Was she—also a dream?"

"Who?"

Los did not reply. His head sank back and he closed his eyes.

Gusev looked through all the peep-holes in turn. There was nothing but darkness. Drawing the blanket over his shoulders, he sat hunched under it. He had no wish to think, remember, or dream. What was the use? The metal egg droned and vibrated drowsily as it sped through the bottomless void.

Time, infinite, not of the Earth, lagged interminably. Gusev sat hunched in a torpor. Los was asleep. The chill of eternity settled like invisible dust on his heart and mind.

Suddenly a blood-curdling scream rent the air. Gusev jumped to his feet, his eyes popping from his head. Los was standing among his scattered blankets, his gauze bandage hanging over his face, and shouting madly:

"She's alive!"

He lifted his bony hands and began to pound and claw at the leather-bound wall.

"She's alive! Let me out—I'm choking—she was, she was!"

He thrashed about and shouted for a long time, then fell back limply, spent, in Gusev's arms. Gradually he calmed down and dozed off again.

Gusev huddled under the blanket again. Every desire he had had turned into ashes; he felt numb. His ears had grown accustomed to the metallic pulsation of the spaceship and unconscious of any other sounds. Los muttered and moaned in his sleep; every now and then his face lit up with joy.

Gusev looked down at his sleeping companion and thought:

"You're doing the right thing, dear man. Don't bother to wake up, just go on sleeping. When you wake up, you'll sit hunched under your blanket like me, shivering like a crow on a frozen stump. Is this the end?"

He did not even bother to close his eyes. He just sat and looked at a gleaming nail in front of him. He was completely indifferent, sinking into oblivion.

More time, vast quantities of it, elapsed in this manner.

Suddenly he heard strange sounds of something knocking and scraping against the iron shell.

Gusev opened his eyes. He was coming out of his coma. He listened. It sounded as though they were driving through mounds of pebble and debris. Something fell on the ship and slipped down its side. There was more scrapping and scratching. Now something struck the other side, and the ship shook. Gusev roused Los. They crawled to the observation tubes and gasped.

All around them in the dark were fields of chipped fragments that glittered like diamonds. Stones, rocks and crystals sparkled with long pointed rays. And a long way off, the shaggy sun hung in the black night.

"We are passing through the head of a comet, I think," whispered Los. "Switch on the rheostats. We must get out of this field, or the comet will draw us to the sun."

Gusev climbed to the top peep-hole and Los stood by the rheostats. The scratching and grating increased. Gusev shouted from above:

"Easy now, there's a rock on our right. Put her on as far as she'll go. A mountain—there's a mountain coming at us. That'll do. We've passed it. Let her go, man, let her go!"

THE EARTH

The diamond fields were the trail of a comet speeding through space. For a long time the ship, drawn into its gravitational field, pushed through the meteoritic cloud. Its speed increased and the absolute laws of mathematics followed their course—gradually the paths of the ship and the meteorites changed direction, fanning out at an ever-widening angle. The golden haze—the head of the unknown comet—and its tail—the streams of meteorites—were shooting along a hyperbola, a hopeless curve, to skirt the sun and disappear for ever in space. The ship's curve of flight now approached an ellipsis.

The wild hope of returning to Earth resuscitated the two men. They kept their eyes glued to the peep-holes. The ship's side facing the sun was hot. They threw off their clothes.

The diamond fields were far beneath them now. A glittering mass at first, they soon faded into a grey-white veil and vanished. Then the opalescent Saturn appeared away in the distance, ringed by its satellites.

The egg, attracted by the comet, was returning to the solar system.

A little later the obscurity was pierced by a shining line, which soon dimmed and disappeared. It was a swarm of asteroids—little planets—spinning round the sun. The force of their gravity increased the curve of the egg's flight. Then Los saw a strange shiny narrow sickle through the top peep-hole. It was Venus. Almost simultaneously Gusev, at the other peep-hole, gasped and turned a perspiring red face to Los.

"It's her, honestly, it's her! . . ."

A silvery-blue globe was shining warmly in the murky blackness. On one side of it a tiny ball, no bigger than a currant, gleamed brightly. The ship was speeding somewhat off course, and Los decided upon a dangerous measure--turning the neck of the ship around to deflect the combustion axis from the trajectory of the flight. He was successful. The direction changed. The warm little ball gradually climbed to the zenith.

Space and time fled on and on. Los and Gusev clung to the observation tubes and reeled back on to their scattered fur rugs and blankets again and again. Their strength was giving out. They were dying of thirst, but the water supply had run out.

Suddenly, in a semi-coma, Los saw the furs, blankets and bags floating along the walls. Gusev's half-naked body hung in the air. It was like a nightmare. Gusev was now lying next to a peep-pole. He picked himself up, mumbling to himself, clutching at his breast and shaking his curly head. Tears coursed down his face and drooping moustache.

"Our own, our very own dear Earth!"

Through the mist of his consciousness Los realized that the ship had turned neck foremost, attracted by the Earth. He crawled to the rheostats and pulled at them—the egg began to vibrate and roar. He bent to look through a peep-hole.

There, hanging in the darkness, was the huge watery globe, bathed in sunshine. Its oceans were blue, and the contours of its islands green. Clouds spread over one of its continents. The moist globe was turning slowly. The tears welling up in their eyes prevented the men from seeing it. Singing with love, their hearts flew out to meet the bluish moist shaft of light. The land of humanity! The flesh of life! The heart of the world!

The globe of the Earth now covered half the sky. Los pulled the rheostats as far as they would go. The ship was still flying too fast—the casing was hot, the rubber lining inside and the leather upholstery were smouldering. Summoning all his remaining strength Gusev shifted the lid over the porthole. An icy gust swept in through the aperture. The Earth opened its arms to receive its prodigal sons.

The impact was shattering. The spaceship's shell cracked. The egg dived deep into a grassy mound.

It was noon of Sunday, June third. On the shore of Lake Michigan, a great distance from where the spaceship finally dropped, people who were out boating, lounging in open-air restaurants and cafés, playing tennis, golf and football, and flying kites in the cloudless sky—all these crowds of holiday-makers who had come to the lovely green lake shore to enjoy their weekend amid the rustling June foliage, heard a strange whining sound that lasted a full five minutes.

World war veterans scanned the sky and remarked that heavy shells made that sort of whining sound. Then many saw an egg-shaped shadow flit rapidly over the ground.

Within an hour a great crowd had gathered round the damaged spaceship. People came flocking from all directions, climbing over fences, riding in cars, plying the blue lake in row boats. The egg, smeared with soot and grease, dented and cracked, stood listing to one side on a mound. Many conjectures were formed, one more absurd than the other. The people grew especially excited when they noticed the inscription on the half-open lid over the porthole, which read: "RSFSR. Took off from Petrograd, August 18, 192. . ." It was all the more surprising since it was now June

3, 19. . . In a word, the inscription had been made three and a half years before.

Suddenly the crowd heard faint moans issuing from the interior of the mysterious apparatus. They backed away in silence and consternation. A squad of policemen, a doctor and twelve newspapermen with cameras appeared on the scene. They opened the porthole and carefully lifted out two half-naked human bodies. One was emaciated, thin as a skeleton, old and white-haired—and unconscious. The other, with a bleeding face and broken arms, was moaning pitifully. Exclamations of sympathy and concern burst from the crowd. The celestial travellers were deposited in a car and driven to a hospital.

A bird outside the window was singing in a voice crystal with joy. It sang of sunbeams, and of the blue sky. Los lay back on his pillows listening. Tears streamed down his haggard face. He had heard that crystal voice somewhere. But where?

Beyond the curtains flapping gently in the morning breeze, sparkled dew-bedecked blades of grass. The wet leaves cast playful shadows on the curtains. The bird chirruped.

In the distance, a white cloud was rising from behind the forest.

Someone's heart was pining for this earth, for the clouds, the pattering rains and sparkling dew, the giants wandering over the green hills. He remembered—it was a bird which had sung like this of Aelita's dreams on a sunny morning, far away from the Earth. Aelita.... But had she existed at all? Or was she only a dream? No. The bird was singing in its chirping language of the time when a woman, blue as dusk, with a thin little sad face, sat at a fire and sang an old old song of love.

That was why the tears were streaming down Los's sunken cheeks. The bird was singing of the one who had remained beyond the stars, and of the grey wizened old dreamer who had traversed the skies.

The curtain flapped gently in the wind. The aroma of honey, earth and moisture crept into the room.

On one such morning Skiles turned up at the hospital. He shook Los's hand vigorously—"Congratulations, old man"—then sat down on a stool beside the bed and pushed his hat to the back of his head.

"Doesn't look as though the trip's agreed with you, old man," he said. "I've just seen Gusev. He's a brick: arms in plaster casts, jaw broken, and cheerful as the day. Tickled pink to be back. I sent his wife a wire and five thousand dollars. I've also wired my newspaper about you—you've got a pot of money waiting for you for your 'Travel Notes.' But you'll have to improve your machine—you made a bum landing! To think that almost four years have passed since that crazy evening in Petrograd! How about a glass of brandy, my boy,—it'll pep you up."

Skiles went on chattering, casting cheerful and solicitous glances at the patient. His face was sun-tanned and genial and his eyes were full of avid curiosity. Los held out his hand.

"I'm glad to see you, Skiles."

THE VOICE OF LOVE

Snowflakes danced over Zhdanov Embankment, swept over the sidewalks, whirled round the swinging street-lamps. They blanketed the doorways and window ledges, and, borne by the blizzard, moaned and raged in the park beyond the river.

Los strode down the embankment holding his collar up against the wind. His warm scarf fluttered behind his back, the snow pricked his face and his feet slipped over the ice on the road. He was returning to his solitary flat after his day's work at the factory. The people in the district were accustomed to the sight of his broad-brimmed hat, his scarf wound round his chin, his stooped shoulders, and even, when he bowed in greeting, letting the wind ruffle his white hair, to the strange look in his eyes which had seen what no other man had witnessed before him.

At another time, perhaps, some young poet would have been inspired by his odd figure with the fluttering scarf, wandering through the snowstorm. But times were different: poets were no longer captivated by snowstorms, or stars, or lands beyond the clouds. They were fired by the pounding of the hammers throughout the country, the humming of saws, the rustling of sickles, the wheezing of scythes—the buoyant songs of the Earth.

It was six months since Los had returned to Earth. The interest which the first telegram had evoked in the world, announcing the arrival of two men from Mars, had subsided. Los and Gusev had eaten the required number of dishes at one hundred and fifty banquets, suppers and scientific gatherings. Gusev had wired Masha to come to him from Petrograd, dressed her up like a doll, had given several hundred interviews, bought himself a motor-cycle, wore round goggles and spent six months touring America and Europe, telling all and sundry about his battle with the Martians, about the spiders and the comets, and the way he and Los had almost landed on the Big Dipper. Then, returning to Soviet Russia, he founded a "society for dispatching military detachments to the planet of Mars for the purpose of saving the remnants of its toiling population."

Los was building a universal motor of the Martian type at one of the engineering plants in Leningrad.

At six p.m. he usually went home, ate in solitude, and before going to bed took up a book—but the poet's lines and the fantasies of the novelist seemed like childish prattle to him. Turning off the light, he would lie gazing into the darkness, and his lonely thoughts would flow on and on. . . .

Los made his way along the embankment at the usual hour Clouds of snow swirled up into the heights, into the raging blizzard.

Snowflakes drifted off the cornices and roofs of the buildings. The street lamps rocked. Los found it hard to breathe.

He stopped in his tracks and raised his head. The wind had torn the stormy clouds. A star twinkled in the bottomless pit of the black sky. Los gazed at it with wild yearning—its ray had pierced his heart. "Tuma, Tuma, star of sorrow." The ragged edges of the clouds veiled the abyss again, shutting out the star. In that brief moment a vision which had always eluded him now flashed through his mind with terrible clarity.

. . . He had heard a noise—like the angry buzzing of bees—in his sleep. Then there was a loud rapping at the door. Aelita had started, sighed, and begun to shiver. He could not see her in the dark of the cave, only felt her heart beating wildly. The knocks were repeated. Then came Tuscoob's voice: "Take them." Los had drawn Aelita to him. She said, in a barely audible voice:

"Farewell, my husband, Son of the Sky."

Her fingers had slipped over his face. Then Los fumbled for her hand and took the flask with the poison. Very quickly, in a single breath, she murmured into his ear:

"I have been dedicated to Queen Magr. According to our ancient custom, the awful Law of Magr, a virgin who has broken her vow is thrown into the well of the labyrinth. You have seen it. But I could not deny myself the love of the Son of the Sky. I am happy. I thank you for having given me life. You have returned me to the millennium of Khao. Thank you, my husband."

Aelita kissed him, and he smelled the bitter odour of the poison on her lips. Then he drank the rest of the dark liquid—there was still enough of it in the flask. Aelita had just touched it with her lips. The rapping on the door made Los get up, but he felt faint, and his hands and legs would not obey him. He returned to the couch, fell over Aelita's body and embraced her. He did not stir when the Martians entered the cave. They tore him from his wife, wrapped her up and bore her away. With a last effort, he had staggered after the skirt of her black cape. There were sparks of fire, and something struck him in the chest and sent him reeling back towards the little golden door of the cave....

Bent against the wind, Los hurried on down the embankment. Then he stopped again, caught in a whirling snow cloud and shouted, as he had that time in the black void of the universe:

"She's alive, alive—Aelita, Aelita!"

The wind snatched up this name, uttered for the first time on Earth, and scattered it amid the whirling snowflakes. Los dug his chin deeper into his muffler, thrust his hands into his pockets and stumped on to his house.

A car was standing at the front door. Little white flies darted in the foggy shafts of its lights. A man in a shaggy fur coat stood stamping the frozen soles of his boots against the sidewalk.

"I've come for you, Mstislav Sergeyevich," he called in a cheerful voice. "Climb in and let's go."

It was Gusev. Hurriedly he explained that at seven in the evening the radio-telephone station was expecting to receive some strange signals of very great force. Nobody could decipher the code. For a week the newspapers in all parts of the world had wondered what the signals meant—it was thought that they came from Mars. The radio station had invited Los to listen in that evening to the mysterious message.

Los got into the car without a word. The white flakes in the cones of light danced frenziedly. The cold wind lashed at his face. The violet lights of the city, the shining lamps along the embankments—lights and more lights—glowed over the snowy desert of the Neva River. In the distance an ice-breaker wailed.

The car drove up to a little round-roofed house standing on a snowy lot at the end of Krasniye Zori Street. The towers and wire nets rising into the snowy clouds hummed desolately. Los opened the snow-coated door, stamped into the warm little house and flung off his scarf and hat. A plump rosy-cheeked man explained something to him, holding his cold red hand in his own warm chubby palms. The hands of the clock were approaching the figure seven.

Los sat down at the wireless and clapped on the earphones. The hand of the clock crawled on. Oh time, the feverish beats of the heart, the icy space of the universe!...

A slow whisper sounded in his ears. Los closed his eyes at once. Again came the distant alarming slow whispering. A strange word was repeated over and over. Los strained his ears. Like a muted bolt of lightning smiting his heart came the distant voice, repeating sorrowfully in an unearthly tone:

"Where are you, where are you, where are you, Son of the Sky?"

The voice died away. Los stared before him with dilated stricken eyes. Aelita's voice. the voice of love and eternity, the voice of yearning, reached him across the universe—calling, begging, imploring: "Where are you, where are you, my love?"